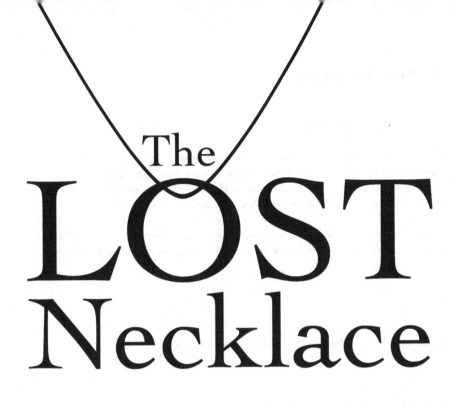

The LOST Necklace

Kuljit Mann

iUniverse®

THE LOST NECKLACE

iUniverse books may be ordered through booksellers or by contacting:

iUniverse
1663 Liberty Drive
Bloomington, IN 47403
www.iuniverse.com
844-349-9409

ISBN: 978-1-6632-1408-9 (sc)
ISBN: 978-1-6632-1409-6 (e)

Print information available on the last page.

iUniverse rev. date: 11/28/2020

DOWNTOWN

WHILE WANDERING IN the Downtown, Ram Singh remembered the morning time. I don't know what to do. God has given so many dollars; God has given me everything; we should thank him. I have worked all my life, and now I have two jobs. Ram Singh was thinking from another point of view. It seemed to him that Pammi did not want to stay at home. She has said many times that she suffocates at home. Ram Singh also spoke to his doctor about it. He had the same idea that Pammi seems to be depressed.

Pammi has a habit from the beginning that she does not take medicine. She drinks liquid medication, but it is tough for her to pass the pill. She will first push the tablet forward with her finger and then drink the water and later feel a shiver.

Ram Singh researched on the internet, but he was not satisfied with anything. He wanted to do something for Pammi. He also did not have much faith in allopathic pills. There are side effects to everything, be it a medicine or a lot of work. Pammi was stubborn. When the girl went to Windsor University, Pammi had a bed in her heart. The girl's education would be incomplete without her. There was a delusion in her thoughts.

Equity in the home was such that there was never a shortage. Education Savings Plan money is available.

Student loans could be taken if required, but who will explain to Pammi?

Ram Singh's thought was that Pammi should be happy, but how could she be satisfied? He always tried to talk to sad women. He was trying to find out about them. Many beautiful girls were also low. He would try to find out the cause of their sadness.

In Downtown, he found a young beggar. Her name was Perry. Homeless Perry also had a dog named Agnes. Agnes always clings to Perry as if trying to comfort her.

She would sit in one of the corners around the Dundas circle. Don't ask for anything from anyone; have an empty coffee cup in front of people who will put something in it. She wouldn't even say thank you. As if saying that you have to give, if not, then get away. Ram Singh occasionally looked at Perry and Agnes when he was not busy with a hot dog cart.

She would occasionally come to his cart, picking up hot dogs and sausages for Agnes. He had never had a soft drink to drink. Ram Singh found out that she doesn't buy soft drinks just for money. After eating hot dogs, she would drink water from a washroom. Perry herself said. Whatever one does, a can of coke is worth a dollar, and a bottle of water is also worth a dollar.

Perry would occasionally sit in a corner next to Ram Singh's cart. Begging is also a job, never sitting in begging and smoking; whenever she wants to smoke, she would get up and walk away. She would pull the last drag hard and come back to Agnes.

Her jeans were torn above the knees, unknown that jeans are too old or she had torn it from there knowingly. There would be a glimpse of her white thighs from the potty spot, and the passer-by would get more emotional.

Such a situation arises in a beautiful girl.

She is, and life does not know what has become of her. The body was heavy, which can be called sexy. Sadness on her face and half-dressed clothes, just sitting in the Downtown or walking around looking like a beggar, and that was her skill. In a way, she was good at her job if I had to read from a different view.

Ram Singh does not know why he wanted to know about her life. Maybe in her story, he finds some clues to please Pammi. Perry would be less than thirty, perhaps even less than twenty-five, but she wasn't over thirty at all. Pammi was now over fifty but seemed to be around sixty.

Perry slowly walked, the hot dog cart came, and she ordered the hot dog and asked, "Mr. Ram, you look happy today?"

"Yes, Perry, I'm better today than ever before because my daughter is coming from Windsor today and will be home on the weekend. This evening we will have the whole family sitting together and talking a lot."

"Oh, great, very nice."

"After all, Christmas is coming. Happiness is slowly coming to everyone. Aren't you happy?" Ram Singh said.

Perry laughed, "That's me too."

"Are you going to visit your family at Christmas too?" It was a question that Ram Singh should not have asked, but he did ask today.

"No, Ram Singh, I'm not going anywhere. Christmas will also pass around Dundas with Agnes. After all, people are very kind at Christmas. A few extra dollars, I would buy a nice snack for Agnes. He also needs a jacket in the cold, and he's too tired to eat sausages every day."

"Good Perry, I'm leaving early today. If you need anything, tell me. I'll make sausages for Agnes for free.

"Yes, yes, why not? your daughter is coming today; you are glad to want to share happiness with Agnes, that is great, you will give free today, God bless her."

Ram Singh locked the cart and covered it with tarpaulin. He took out some essentials, which he had to take home in a van, and put in the freezer. Besides, he used to come on weekends, even though most of the offices were closed, but there were still enough visitors, and his work was as usual."

"Bye, Perry. Bye, Agnes." Ram Singh put the goods in the van and drove away. Perry took care of the sausage. It was not time to give it to Agnes.

Ram Singh took a four-twenty-seven highway off the Gardner Express Highway and drove out to Derry. He remembered that Pammi's depression medicine was over. There was no prescription, so I called the doctor and had it faxed. The mixture was ready, and he took it and walked home again.

Ram Singh had turned on the radio, but his attention was not on the radio at all. He started thinking about Pammi. What kind of disease have poor women contracted? It has been four years since she started taking depression pills. It was no longer a matter of depression but medicine. If she doesn't take or misses, she can't get out of bed the next day—the air in the skull slides and cracks. The doctor says it will go away slowly. The body has become used to a toxic chemical. Medicine becomes the need of her body. Besides, Ram Singh advises, she never stops working, never even missed overtime when asked.

Everything would be fine, but she digs out a reason to believe that they need money for this reason or that reason. She feels insecure and thinks she is very miserable.

'Are you alone miserable?' Ram Singh thought all the time.

And what about the pain, what about the weight on your soul? Everything is good, and she is worried about anything.

Ram Singh is talking in his thoughts. The time has come now. I have to do something to make her understand. Maybe I would seek help for my daughter.

It's a four-hour drive; he reached home at three-thirty.

When the van stopped, the phone rang; he put his ear to it, and then Babu said, "Hi Dad."

"That babu, where are you?" When will you arrive? I have just arrived home; your mother would be waiting for you."

"Oh, Dad, I think you miss Mom so much, so talk to Mom now."

"Yes, are you here?" Pammi asked on the phone.

"Where are you, both of you? When did Babu come?"

"She arrived at ten o'clock. I was surprised. She never woke up early usually but today

Babu left at six o'clock, drank coffee on the way. We are at Fortino now, and we are taking the cake for you."

"Why the cake?"

"I also asked, saying Dad likes it and I have to buy it with my own money, now I'm working… part-time."

Ram Singh laughed and said, "How long are you coming? I will make you some tea; Babu will not drink tea I know; tell her to get Tim Horton for her."

"Yes, we'll get there in ten minutes; we are already with the cashier."

It was mid-December, and most offices were closing. The downtown rush was slowing down. Tourists also rarely come these days; only locals go around to see the lights, but they seldom get out of the car at the hot dog cart and what someone has to eat. Ram Singh also had to come in a couple of days. He did not know why he gets a glimpse of Babu from Perry, probably because they are the same age. He had been preparing the ground for several days to talk to Perry. It wasn't Perry; it was Babu. He did not want Babu to ever find herself in a situation where her mother was coming out of it or seeing a glimpse of Perry.

Perry took the hot dog and said, "Ram Singh, I see that you are showing some sympathy, and I am irritated by the sympathy. My father had the same sympathy. Only empathy can break your back. Like a toy given to a child."

"My daughter, I'm not sympathetic; I'm just asking if I can get some help for my own family.."

"I'm not your daughter, don't call me daughter anymore; there are many more hot dog carts."

Perry was angry.

"What can I tell you?"

"Anything but no more, daughter."

"Come on, Miss Perry, you are my friend, just friend, now tell me something about yourself."

"You have to close your cart. Can you afford this?"

"If you say so, I'll throw the cart in the garbage."

Perry laughed and said, "No, it's not necessary.

Let's put the tarpaulin on now. I'll see how much damage it can do to listen."

Ram Singh immediately locked the cart.

"I couldn't sleep all night when my dad took me to a psychiatrist, and he declared my postpartum depression in my report."

"What is this postpartum depression?" Ram Singh asked.

"I had a son, and he was four months old. I don't know who his father is. My thoughts became such that I could hurt him. I can even kill him. I can commit suicide and don't know what to do, and I can't be allowed to be open. The doctor also sent the report to the health department, and the ambulance picked me up. That's when the only thing that came to my mind was that if anyone wants to erase my name from this world, he can only be my dad."

"I am sorry, Perry." Ram Singh said briefly.

"No, Ram Singh, there is nothing wrong on your part; you are not part of that world, I feel it. I am worried about my son that something might happen to him, and the doctor was saying that I was a danger to him. I have nightmares; my son is hungry, he has a cold, he has no clothes. I was being treated in my father's shelter and could do nothing for my child. It dawned on me that my son was about to be killed and that I could not save him as a mother."

"But how did the idea come to your mind that your dad is your enemy? I'm a dad, too; it can never happen; you must have misunderstood somewhere."

"You don't know Ram Singh, you are from another country, you are different people, we are not like you, we are good, but we are different, and Dad will definitely not be like you, you love your daughter very much."

"Perry, I can say for sure that no matter what the country is, where a border starts and where a border ends, dads all over the world are the same who want the best for their children."

Perry laughed and said, "Ram Singh, how can you be so sure when you don't know anything? If you want to hear it, listen, don't waste time with your meaningless views. it's going to be lunch, and that's the rush hour for me and for you too."

"Okay, Perry, don't talk anymore; you do continue your story-thing."

"I don't know why I wanted to breastfeed my son. Maybe this is the divine instinct of motherhood. It was my fundamental right, but my dad didn't like it either. How did he create the conspiracy? I don't know? I just became hyper, even hyper watchful; I don't know what was in it. Even if the wax stops, your figure will deteriorate. No one cared about my brain, which was deteriorating. "own."

"Now the same mother and the same father come after me, and I go out in front of people knowing how to tease them. You know that I don't need to earn enough. Agnes is the only one who lives with me, for when I have some money, I become carefree. My mother once grabbed my arm in Dundas Square. There was a good commotion, even the police came. She wanted to give me a letter of revenue agency, and I was saying that I was homeless. Go and tell the revenue people too. The police, seeing my condition, sent my mother back with some explanation and some laws. She could not do that with an adult. That night, for the first time, I put on a marijuana suit and slept soundly. Now I have no dreams. Never Not that I forgot to laugh, no... Ram Singh now, but I forgot to cry. This naughty Agnes keeps making me laugh. If I tell you what he did, you will be amazed."

"Yeah yeah ... Perry tell me how Agnes makes you laugh too?"

"Agnes knows that after Mariuana drags, I have a sound sleep.

He also knows where the money bag is. He keeps an eye on the biker whenever he comes. Seeing him, he pulls the package and then hits me; I know right away that David has arrived. Once you know what happened? When David arrived, I was in the Eaton Center washroom, and we were camping just outside Burger King. Agnes surrounded David's bicycle. Don't let him go ahead; happily scare him anyway.

I handed over to Miller, my homeless friend, got rid of him, and crossed the road right after David, not seeing him stop and fell at his feet. He also understood and laughed a lot. Agnes stopped him for ten minutes. With such a bond, David can now borrow, but I never hit his money. He knows, and so does Agnes. There are many more stories about Agnes, my dear baby. With that, Perry kissed Agnes on the mouth.

Now Perry was silent as if he had told the outline; then Ram Singh should understand everything on the graph.

Why? Why did you keep quiet? Is that all there is to it? I can say for sure that you are the daughter of a good family, then this bagging?"

"Looks like Ram Singh, you don't understand me."

"Flatly, I don't understand."

"Do you know why I live downtown?"

"No"

"A downtown is a place where everyone has in common; every town has its own Downtown that is always moving with the times. In downtown Toronto, people from all over the world can easily fit. Tourists, traders, shopkeepers, and even beggars like me. I have never been hurt by the people here. He who does not give anything to beggars does not feel ashamed; he goes ahead, saying sorry. This is what I want. Thoughts do not live in our homes and people. These are the thoughts that children follow.

These thoughts killed my only son. No one in the house is free. My mother, my father, my brother, are slaves of all houses. No one lives one's life."

How is that, Perry?"

Before Perry could answer, a woman came and stopped. She was nicely dressed, and she hugged Perry. Perry stood up and said, "Oh my God, Lisa, are you still at work today?"

"Yes, Sweetie, I had to come. There was an assignment pending. The Ross & Ross loan consignment is due in the first week of January. Hi Agnes, how are you?" Agnes slapped Lisa's feet with her paws, wagging her tail and placing her front paws on her knees. Lisa sat down and fell in love with Agnes.

"Lisa, this is my friend Ram Singh."

"Yes, I know, his hot dogs are very tasty. I don't know if he got Indian sauce; it's just great." Hi ... Ram Singh." Lisa shook hands with Ram Singh.

"How many more days are you coming, Lisa?"

"That's it; today I finished my work. I am going to Berry this evening with Smith. The rest of the time, we will spend our time there, maybe we would go to Orillia to meet Smith's mother. Now you tell me what I would bring for you and Agnes from Berry."

"Agnes needs a dog jacket, Lisa, from Berry or Toronto does not matter."

"Sure, I'll take it, but for you?"

"That's all, don't put any more burden on you."

"Perry, I am going to get coffee. Will you take it?"

"Yes, Lisa, single sugar double cream for me, a Swiss sandwich for Agnes and a steep tea for Ram Singh, he doesn't drink coffee."

"Okay, Perry."

After Lisa left, Ram Singh asked, "How do you know I don't drink coffee and drink tea?"

"Ram Singh, this is my home around Downtown; I know everything. You bring a thermos full of tea from home, but I'm sorry you never reconciled me."

"That naughty girl, I didn't even know I was from your downtown; I'm sorry, I'll bring you some tea from now on."

"Yes, that's right, tea and brown bread for the future."

Ram Singh laughed and said, "Those are called Parantha; I will bring those too, now we have become friends."

"Yes, Ram Singh will talk the rest after drinking Lisa's coffee but tell me one thing too; what do you think is called home?"

"The house is the house; what is there to tell?"

That's when Lisa arrived. Perry got up, took a tray of coffee from her, and said goodbye. Perhaps this behavior of her had something to do with Ram Singh.

Lisa opened her wallet and pulled out a $20 note and handed it to Perry.

"No, Lisa, I won't take it. You don't even have the excuse that it's Christmas. I told you my need, I don`t need the money and what should I do? You know, I don't even drink, because Agnes doesn't like it. I have enough money to give to David, so say goodbye to Smith on my behalf."

Lisa put the money back in her purse. Saying Merry Christmas, she walked to the subway train station.

"Yes, we were talking about home."

"Before you tell any further, tell me what's wrong with your drink and Agnes?"

Perry laughed and said, "It's exciting. One evening I had a drink. I just drank neat, and I became hyper, began to speak loud and nonsense. It was ten o'clock at night, and I fell on the road. No car was coming, and I fell in the middle of the road. Agnes' leash was clutched in my hand. Agnes couldn't move, just barked. Hearing its barking and seeing a girl fall on the road, a car stopped. He came and shook me, but I was unconscious, and Agnes's rope was wrapped around my arm. He somehow made me stand up. I also looked at him at dawn and called him. Thank you. Seeing my smile, he understood something else, and he started stroking my limbs. Just then, Agnes got angry and bit him on the heel. He bit so hard that he bled. Leaving me, he got into the car and ran.

I fell to my knees and fell asleep in my sleeping bag. I don't even think Agnes is sitting alone in the cold outside." Perry laughed.

"What's so funny about that?" Ram Singh said.

"I'll tell you... tell you." She starts laughing loudly and puts her hands on her sides, can`t control. He laughs and, after a while said, "Now when

Agnes saw anybody with LCBO bag, he starts barking at. Now when I saw anybody carry an LCBO bag, I hold the leash tightly.

The throat gets sore. If I see someone in the distance with an envelope, I will snatch Agnes."

"Wow, that's amazing; Agnes is doing social work. Don't drink.

Perry became serious and said, "Ram Singh, you tell me, if I can stop drinking at Agnes' request, then why couldn't I quit at my father's request?"

Ram Singh had no readymade answer and shrugged.

"I tell you, Ram Singh, the Dad, didn't know how to talk to me. Agnes knows how to talk to me. Dad's house is too small, but my house is too big." Perry was silent for a few seconds and then said, "Ram Singh, are you and your family living your life?" Have you not become slaves of the house? You mentioned that your daughter is studying at Windsor University. Have you left her alone with a leash around her neck and sent her to university?"

"I don't understand."

"No one understands Ram Singh. You are not ignorant; you are deceitful; you are hypocritical. My father is also a hypocrite. I gave up his hypocrisy, and he is bothered by my begging. That's why I beg. Lisa has told me once or twice that she can arrange a job, but I refused.

Dad is from Halifax, and my mother is Italian. Is there a match? But when they got married, agreements were reached, and new thinking was born. I was born after thinking. Don't come, don't do that... You don't do the same with your girl? ... Ram Singh became silent. The answer was not thinking If ...

Why are you silent now?"

"Perry, I don't have the answer to any of your questions. I disagree with you, but there is no answer, I don't understand, who is right and who is wrong?"

Perry laughed and said, "Old man, is that what my dad does that you do?" Nothing exactly happens. You are right or wrong. After my one move after another, Dad used to say the same thing. Let's not do it again. No one is asking where I was already wrong? Also, what is the homework to make your girl just like you? Why don't you let someone live his or her life?"

"Perry, you talk very wisely but have you ever thought that you could tell people these things, explain them, and for that, you have to change your lifestyle?"

"Ram Singh it is very easy to talk. Answer one thing. You have a daughter; what will you do if someone kills her?"

Ram Singh thought for a moment and said, "I don't know, how can that thinking flourish when it hasn't happened?"

"Ram Singh, if this happens, you cannot become a social reformer and say, 'Those people, don't kill anyone's daughter.' People will call him crazy if he does this.

"Ram Singh, my son was born. At first, they used to ask for an abortion. I don't know who the father is. Yes, I didn't know who his father was, but my family knew I was his mother. It was my choice or an event, but he was my son.

What right does anyone have to impose something on me to the point?

My son dies because of their ideals. My son dies because his mother is not there to look after him.

How will they take care of my son?

They can't take care of themselves.

I also saw that whenever Dad is absent from home, he has to tell Mom the reason. Same thing with Mom, why they explain to each other?

Why tell each other? Sure they don't trust the world. I do not understand. Do you do the same, Ram Singh?"

Ram Singh was still confused, and he was just looking for an opportunity for his Pammi's life and happiness. He did not know from which mountains Perry descended.

Seeing him silent, Perry said again, "Stress and despair. Millions of people die every night and come back to life in the morning to die again." People have learned to cope with this despair and are now teaching their children to cope. It is only because of the overdose of depression that people like me do drugs and can do anything under the influence of drugs.

Why don't they think that an overdose should not be given?

Do you mention that your wife is depressed?"

"Yes, Perry said, she's been depressed for years."

"What are you doing?"

"She takes medicine."

"Ever wondered why she is depressed?

"No"

"I'll tell you why she's sick."

"Yes, suggest me," said Ram Singh with a faint smile.

"She is definitely not living her life. It looks like you never gave her a chance. You are scared people."

"I can say for sure that a weak person like you will make his daughter sick too. What will he takes care of his daughter if he can't take care of his wife?" That's because you believe in more medicine than their lives."

As she spoke, Perry was tense, with frowns on her forehead. Seeing her, Agnes began to bark. First slowly and then in the whole dog, lute. He wanted to get free from Perry. Agnes wanted to attack the situation that makes Perry sad.

Perry was holding him tightly. Ram Singh got up and stood up and realized the danger. He slipped back a little in fear. Seeing Ram Singh move back, Agnes began to growl even more angrily. Perry's grip was weakening. Perry realized. She suddenly started laughing. Laughing, he said to Ram Singh, "Ram Singh Start Laughing, Laugh Without reason." Agnes understands that language."

Frightened, Ram Singh started laughing. Laughing faintly first and then a little darker, Perry stepped forward, slapped Ram Singh's hand, and laughed openly. Agnes was also judging the situation and thought Perry is happy now.

Seeing Perry, Agnes took a deep breath and sat down to rub Perry's feet.

SELF-WRINKLES

JOGI WAS NOT trained to dance at all, never learned from anywhere, but he felt that he could dance with Helen. Helen was aware of him and his way of life. His style was different, but at first, Jogi found Raman in her. Gradually Raman became hostile, and Helen became overwhelmed. They just came to celebrate today. Jogi was pleased as if his hopes had been dashed, and this dusk would change his life. It seemed to him that the artist inside him would die, like many artists, but Helen made him make money.

After a long time today, his soul was dancing. Dancing is done by the soul, and it comes to the body by itself. Helen brought another drink and drank as she danced. Helen looked deeply at him. She wanted to see him happy. She went to the music desk. As the English song ended, the Punjabi song "Dil Tote Tote Ho Gaya" resounded throughout the hall.

"Do you want to increase my self-confidence?" Jogi said, looking at Helen with drunken eyes.

"Come on," Helen didn't answer and started dancing like a squirrel.

Looking at these two and listening to the Punjabi song, people came to the dance floor, and it seemed that this song would continue all night. People were still ready to dance with Jogi. With yesterday's show, it appeared that Toronto had found a new star in stand-up comedy with new styles and new things. Instant comedy is a favorite of the people, and it is not an onion farm. Still, Jogi smashed a lot of melons in yesterday's program.

Jogi noticed something and asked Helen, "Do you think I'm dancing well?"

"What is your problem?"

"What?"

"You don't come out of yourself. As long as you don't come out of yourself, there will be no dancing in you."

"I am learning with effort."

"Jogi, art never comes with learning; comedy is in your blood, that's why people have accepted you. Tell me, do you like me?"

"Yes, your white color is in my blood."

"Just thinking that I am white, my lips look sexy to you, and you have to go for this color, as soon as this thing climbs on your head, your soul will dance." You will only see me, you will not see anyone else, and that will be the first step of your dance, later you will dance.

"OK, boss."

Helen also got heavy feet and started talking, and they walked towards the table.

"Jogi, I don't understand why you asked this question when you are high?"

"Just like that. No logical reason."

"No, nothing like that happens in life. There must be a reason behind everything. Let us go now; you have ruined my whole mood."

Jogi got up as if he had answered Helen and came out of the bistro.

"I didn't want to upset you, I just wanted to learn to dance, and that's why my next play, in which my role is like this."

"Jogi, sometimes I think my son did something wrong brought you to me for the introduction. Maybe he thinks differently."

"I don't know; maybe you figure out yourself."

"Are we going home, Helen?"

"Is there another place? We drank as much as we afford."

"What, do we ran out of money? Oh, my God?"

"No, I put the money in the fridge."

Jogi assumed, "I don't intend to go home, my heart is pounding, my heart wants to embrace the whole world, but one thing I don't understand is why Mike didn't come with us?" He is silent, too; I am afraid of his silence.

Helen kept quiet and kept driving. Her car was over speeding. She could be charged or get an accident, but Jogi didn't think it appropriate to say anything; He knew that this white, velvety, and beautiful woman would not listen to him.

When they got home, it was two o'clock in the morning. The house was moving, and Mike was awake.

Seeing Mike awake, Helen came out and lit a cigarette, took a long puff. She was thinking.

Jogi came out and, seeing Helen's mood, went to his room and lay down on the bed. I could not sleep.

'Can I dance? Can I get into a character that I am not?' He was thinking.

Yesterday was rehearsal again, and he had to show some of his steps in this rehearsal too.

He remembered his director's words - the artist is the one who changes his existence, not only clothes. Whatever it is, you are not an artist. Last time he also said that fake pistols do not work, only real firearms the audience will like to see. He will control the bullet's sound with the music but bring the real pistol without the shell.

"Just then, there was a movement outside, and he became alert. Mike and Helen were arguing. It was now a daily routine.

He met Mike in a mall, Curled up with a cold. At that time, Jogi was working part-time in a barbershop. In front of his shop, Mike was begging from the people. Whenever he had enough money for mickey, he would go to the LLCBO by liquor drink and sleep somewhere. Do it again after two or three hours.

Mike saw Jogi looking at him and approached him and said, "You'll have twenty dollars, it's freezing today, and I want to spend the night in a motel."

"I don't have twenty, only five dollars if your work goes well ..." Mike walked away after hearing, without giving any response.

Jogi remembered that his wife had kept old jackets in the trunk of the car for donation. He followed Mike and said, "I have warm jackets; if you need in this weather, I'd be happy if you could like and take one."

15

"Oh, sure, that would be great."

Mike and Jogi walked towards the car, opened the trunk, and Mike turned around, took a knee-length jacket, put it on, and walked away without saying a word. Jogi found it strange that he didn't even say thank you.

Mike zipped up as he walked and buttoned up and covered his head with the hoodie. He was feeling warm or not, but Jogi felt his warmth, and he was delighted.

From then on, Mike and Jogi started saying hello every day. Mike walked around the plaza all day, but he was clean and tidy the next day. He seemed to have taken a shower.

One day the Jogi was idle. The owner of the shop, seeing the work was done, asked him to leave. Instead of going home, he wanted to talk to Mike, and he said to Mike, "Let's get in the car."

"No, my Mickey's money is not enough yet."

"It doesn't matter; I'll buy Mickey for you." Jogi was greedy. He was looking for a character who would run away like Mike.

What else did Mike want? He said `yes` and they took Mickey and sat in the car. Mike knew what he asks.

"Mike ..."

"Yeah yeah, I know what you have to ask, why I drink so much, you also think I'll sleep on cardboard on the side of the road at night, in the rain and the cold, what is my problem, why I drink all day, and one day I will die. Am I right?"

"Yes, Mike, if you were like this, you would die."

"No, Jogi, my mother will not let me die, and I have no desire to die. I have yet to become a great musician. I play the guitar, drumming classes will start in September, and I will not drink alcohol after that. You know, every plan is set up, so don't worry."

"Doesn't your mother stopping you?"

"Why she advise me to stop? Poking is not a custom among us. I have heard that Asians ruin the lives of their children by over-protecting them.

"How can you say that, Mike?"

"It's a bad thing to interfere in someone's life; look at my mom." These are the days for me to drink alcohol so that I should know how alcoholics feel. I am also a little depressed."

"You can also go to the doctor, get a counselor's advice?"

"Jogi, don't be a Hippocrates, one day you were saying you are an artist; you shouldn't think like that. Twelve days ago, I didn't drink.

I seldom drink now I have free time I have to drink for another forty-two days for fun, and that's it.

Seeing Jogi lost, Mike laughed out loud and said, "I understand what you're thinking.

We can't coin logic on tiny things.

I drink because I'm so bored.

Every morning my health deteriorates; just hangover, but what can I do?

In the next room, my mom sleeps with the one she doesn't like.

"Why"

"Why doesn't she like him?"

"Because he doesn't like me."

"Jogi, I have lost 20 pounds in the last two months. My credit card is in danger; maybe the bank will cancel it. My mom has nothing to give me, so how can she like that man in such a situation?"

"These forty-two days is a short cut for you. During this time, you can also practice guitar, read history about drums; I don't mean to hurt you. Just talk."

After finishing his glass, Mike said, "Good friend, leave me alone, tell me, how is your life?"

"My life could be summed up in two words, entirely different from the rest of Asians.

In India, I belonged to the Drama Art Association and then came to Canada. Like everyone else, I started my life, but the ghost of art did not go away. I know it could swallow my whole life, but my wife could not wait so long, so she returned to India with our son and said that we would come back when you become a great artist. She loves me so much, but she is also a mother. She has to teach our son."

She was a government teacher, and she rejoined. Miss a lot but can't go. Maybe wait a couple more years.

"Just teaching? Your son could go to school. Here. Here in Canada, the school system is better than India."

"Mike, you are not wrong, but you could not get her point. Schooling is not enough."

"All right, leave this crap; I don't want to listen.

"What are the themes of your plays?"

"The same cultural heritage, transmission from generation to generation."

"Great, just like me. Maybe in the future, we can do some joint work. I also have to become an expert in music for a year; then, perhaps I will also get a job in your play.

"Our budget is not that much, Mike."

"I will never be able to call my family here. Maybe they come of their own when our son grows old, or I would visit India, but I don't yet."

I will tell you how to increase the budget; then you can call your family, stay with me. I have plenty of plans."

"OK, I'll go now. If you say so, I can give you a ride."

"No, I will stay here for now. That bastard will still be home. One day I will meet you with my mother

A few days later, Mike came to the joy and said, "That bastard left my mother.

Maybe my mother left him, but he is not in our home now.

Whenever you have time, I will introduce you to my mother.

"I'm too lazy to go today."

"Come on, what time do you leave work?"

"Seven o'clock in the evening."

"OK, I'll see you at seven o'clock, until then I sit in the library."

"Why not bagging today?"

"No, what you said that day is heartwarming, and now I am reading biographies of drummers."

"Great, that's fine for you. Come at seven o'clock. After saying this, Jogi went inside the shop and Mike walked towards the library.

Jogi parked the car in the garage of Mike's house, and they both came out, rang the doorbell and Helen opened the door on the first ring.

"Meet my mom, Helen, and mom; this is Jogi. I talked to you about."

"Nice to see you," said Helen.

"Me Too"

Jogi sat inside, and Mike said, "Mom, you talk, I have to go to Steve, I'll be back in two hours."

"Come soon. We will have dinner as soon as you come."

"Mike was saying that you are an artist and your family moved to India. Such commitment is rarely seen. I wish one day you would become a great artist."

"Thanks, Helen, you are adorable. Just like Mike told me."

"Jogi, just listen to your heart. Forget you have a family, just like Charlie Chaplin, and the heart never cheats. You have talent, I have seen your tube clips. I could not understand the language, but I could observe your acting. Your face looks jolly. These shapes and veins on the front, develop by commitments."

"Helen's shape is in the hands of the artist; I may be wearing a mask-like Charlie. He would laugh and hide his tears in the rain."

"Why don't you come to the big ocean of the mainstream? Mike will support you; I'm with you." I suggest you try stand-up comedy first. You have a wealth of things.

I have watched your videos. Canadians would love such a mixture.

"Thanks, Helen; yes, that's right, one day I will become a good Punjabi artist."

"Why only Punjabi, The Canadian platform embraces every great artist. You should think about something big.

"I have never thought so big; after all, I don't have complete English proficiency."

"It's not about skills; it's about dreams; it's about your directions. Not everyone can become an artist, but everyone can master the language. I can help you with this matter."

"Really?"

"Yes, really, I have my greed in it."

"How is that?"

"Mike wants to be a musician, and if he can pair up with you, his path can be easier, and I can help your pair."

The joy began to think that the straight path is challenging.

Is it even climbing the stairs answers, and who will climb this mountain?

The circus lion also makes many deals; sometimes, you have to take short cuts; just need practice. There is no need to walk alone all your life.

His thinking started trying to find trails.

He will go far away from home by making a short cut.

But what is the concept of home?

Has the Foundation of home nowadays been the one from which culture emerges? If this is the case, then why is Raman scared? Today, to stay at home, one has to live with limited thinking. To save the house, we have to use our 'Bitu' in such a way that he also needs the place to feel fear.

"Yes, Helen, nothing personal, but will you answer me a couple of questions?

"Of course, I do."

"Foundation of the home, nowadays, does not belong to a culture. Is it correct?"

"Jogi I can't say yes or no, simply. We have to communicate with our inners. My concept of a home might be softer than you, or I believe in constant change."

"You mean surrender in totality."

"Again, I would say no simple, yes or no. We have to consider the window of our home, which way that opens. I see through that, but I could not show you my vision, so this is personal. Very personal."

"So, you are surrendering to the situation."

"Yes, I only think about Mike. He is my family, my traditions, culture, everything."

"accepting you in totality, I could not find my answer. If you are right, then why my wife Raman is so scared?"

"Maybe you are doing something, which is not appropriate?"

"No, Helen, nothing like that just untold story. "Sadly, Helen, You are about to forget the way to the house where Raman and Bittu live. Now I want that my son Bittu should learn to scare, the only way for him to feel the need of a home." Raman just cried as she already lost her home forever."

'Hmm'

Helen reached for a glass of water.

"The dialogue of one of my plays was, 'The number of miles sometimes decreases and sometimes increases. He remembered his bit and cried.

"Why does the heart become heavy, Jogi?"

"Thinking about your words, I came up with the idea that I should not disappear. My wife is waiting for me in India. My son must be in school, thinking that his dad is an artist. I am one, and many others like me do not know how to do circus, Helen."

"Yes, Jogi, I also talked to you, thinking of my son. No matter how sincere we may be, there is greed somewhere inside us. I do not force you. No one can force anyone. It is up to our subconscious to support each other."

"Yes, Helen, you are right. To rise high, one has to break oneself. The idol inside can be carved by breaking the extra stone."

"Yes, Jogi, you are right. Just last week, my third boyfriend ran away. It's not his fault, I couldn't hold him. When the heart comes to someone, then the mind does not think of anything. It is not the heart but the brain that works.

Life is simple; it is better to live it as you wish. My mother wanted to join college after I was born, but Dad disagreed with her decision. Densely woven thread, finally broke one day. As time went on, my views on this incident changed, and I finally concluded that both were fine.

The same thing happened to me. Mike's dad left quietly; he didn't share anything. I had a tough week, and then I thought there was something wrong with me that I couldn't make him happy.

He was unhappy, but he never shared his inner. He became so reckless. He loved Mike so much; even then, he could not stop himself. I don't know what I should be supposed to do.

So Jogi doesn't have any questions or answers to everything, sometimes you have to talk to yourself. Life is beautiful; it should be made more attractive."

"Helen, my problem is my culture,

The dilemma follows me. I know that I am an artist, and developing my talent is my devotion, but family life does not leave me behind.

Now I think that if your dreams are different from usual, you should not get married.

Helen paused for a moment and then said, "When you're a kid, you never think anything wrong is going to happen, but it still happens, and it happens to everyone.

The fact is that how to get out of bad times.

I also had a glass house that cracked and shattered. I was still collecting pieces of glass when one night he left, leaving his nine-year-old child behind. Does the child know that his parents are separating? The child does not know that Dad will never be found again

"Yes, Helen, it's tough to share your pillow and blanket with those who wake up in their sleep."

Helen responded, "I had pieces of glass, I had glue, and I rejuvenated Mike,

But what is in my mind? What are my basic needs? I am a woman. I never forget Mike's dad in my life. He is my first love. I wish I could see her before my last breath. Life is so long, how much I already spent how much I still have. I am just a mechanical person."

Mike came and sat down. "Let's have dinner and get a shot or two later," Helen said

"No, Mom, I'm going to bed. I've had dinner; you should have dinner now, I know you are waiting for me as usual."

"Oh, my sweet Miky.."

"Jogi, you should sleep here at night too."

"OK, Mike." Jogi was confused, but he was shocked to hear that he is staying here with Helen.

He became interested in Helen."

After dinner, they went into the room, and Helen said, "Mike is a good guy, he's taking care of his mom, he wants mom to have a good time."

Jogi left his shared apartment and moved in with Mike and Helen, but he hadn't told Raman about it yet. She couldn't get it quickly.

It was Helen's four-bedroom bungalow and was almost free.

Within two months, Jogi began speaking English Fluently. Helen suggested they should start a stand-up comedy show.

The next step for you from stand up comedy is to play or become a rapper if you want. Mike will support you, I guarantee it, and you also promise that you will not leave Mike. If we need money, I could even sell this house for you guys.

Helen was worried that If Jogi stopped here on stand-up comedy, Mike would have no future in One Man Show.

She wanted to get back to the 'Plays as soon as possible. She knew Jogi had immense power to influence the mainstream.

"Mike said your wife is coming to visit this summer."

"Yes, Helen, she loves me, but she loves her son more than me. Maybe they visit for a couple of weeks."

"you have a choice, you can go back to her, but surprisingly it seems different to me or my way of thinking. I want to get back to my shell; I want to find Mike's dad and tell him what I can do for him.

It's also because I have no other choice. My saturation point is to tell Mike's Dad, let's both worry about Mike in the Golden Age."

"Yes, Helen, one day, I would give them a surprise."

"You go around looking for satisfaction by putting something else in your shell. The water has come up, and you're done."

"Yes, Of course.." Jogi smiled.

"Crack-satisfaction? You are now living with me, sleeping with me; Raman did not know this.

you are also insulting the woman in me. Would I like it when my limbs were shattered by Raman's attention looking for her half-man? For God's sake, don't worry about me. You should worry about Raman.

Free her, if you could not tell the truth. She should not be forced to wear a gilt.

"No, Helen, it doesn't happen to us. She can never do wrong."

"My God, do you think this is wrong?" Then why are you doing this?"

"I am a man; even Raman will know somewhere that I can do anything."

"What a bad idea for your wife." Legitimate for you, illegitimate for a woman, coined logic.

Helen, it has been the case with us for centuries.

"We have no time now, but we will talk about this topic again."

"Yes, Helen, we'll talk, but now what?"

"I don't know ..."

"Yes, Helen, where to start."

"Look, I'm a failed woman; I can never freeze the right things. That is why it is my habit to speak right at the wrong time; this habit has become poison for me. How did you think you have the right to sleep with a strange woman, but your wife has no right? She should wait for you for decades and burn her basic instinct to prove her loyalty, shame on you, man."

"Are we celebrating?"

"Of course, we are celebrating but talking about a woman who is helpless, and her basic needs are burning."

"Helen, she is happy, believes me, nothing to worry about."

"Yes, Jogi, give her space; she is a human being; if not, you can't stay at my house."

"I try.

Just phone her in my presence.

"All right. Give me the phone."

Helen and Jogi were celebrating the third stand-up comedy show.

Jogi became hyper with success. It looks like his old arrow is descending. Idle from Helen; he called his wife, Raman.

"Hello"

"Yes, I am speaking, Jogi."

"Sat Sri Akal Deer, but have you forgotten anything today?"

"What"

"You didn't say that, 'my dear Flame'; I'm Jogi. Does it seem that my Flame is Extinguishing!"

Jogi laughed and said, "No, dear, I still want you as much as I did when I was in University. My Raman is full of lust. You are Flame forever."

"Don't lie; We are the best couple of university. We buckled up, emotionally and physically. I know how you make me flamed and call me Lati. I am still your Lati, but why you forgot today. Are you all right. If you say, I could come to you for a while."

"Hold on a minute, dear, someone at the door." Jogi lied.

He was unfortunate. He was dizzy.

It was tough to tell Raman.

How much something crossed his mind in an instant.

In an instant, the entire universe of feelings went through his mind. He thought that if he didn't say it today, it would be even more difficult later. He went to the kitchen and drank half a glass of whiskey at once. He wanted to put an end to that before the tongue trembled. He picked up the phone and said, "Yes, Raman." He fell silent again."

"It seems you are not well. You look very upset. Tell me; I will come for a month."

"No, Lati, I'm fine."

"It feels as if Mother Saraswati has blessed you."

Some of the emotions and some of the intoxication made the Jogi so heavy that his tears flowed.

He stopped somewhere in the solitary hiccups. Helen was looking at him. He looked at Helen and tried to smile and finally smiled. He had not said anything to Raman yet, and he decided to say no. It's as if love, family, and emotions have won, and his desire to be an artist has been lost.

"How is Bittu going to school, Raman?"

"He is OK. You know the studies in Sanawar."

"Ya, I know, expensive school. How you manage, I know. You are great, Raman. Take care of yourself."

"I told you last time I am going to teach, and that keeps me busy all the time. Nowadays, I invite four children who are deficient in maths and call them home and teach them. Their parents ask me for tuition fees, but I wonder what to do with the extra money. They should realize that this noble deed makes me more human.

"Thank God, you are fine and happy."

"But now you never email? Are you busy or angry?"

"I can't find the time; I'm busy with rehearsals. I also joined a drama course at George Brown. Well, now I have to go somewhere and call again."

"Good Dear God Bless You. Raman hung up the phone before hearing the answer.

The dial tone indicates that there is no Raman on the other side.

As soon as he hung up the phone, Jogi unleashed his emotions and started crying loudly.

Helen came and took the yogi in her arms and said, "You have spoken in your language, but still I understand that you could not say what you were supposed to say, is that true?"

Jogi nodded and said yes.

"Jogi, you have to understand what you want. Your double-mindedness will drive you crazy.

Jogi wiped his eyes and said, "I love Raman very much; my veins are looking for her touch; how can I lie to myself and you and Raman."

"Take care, dear, try to understand me."

"Helen, in my college days, I was committed to Theatre. Everybody knew it.

My name was enough for our college drama team. Yearly youth festivals, our plays were appreciated.

That's when Raman met me as a fan and then became an inspiration. She encouraged me, even promoted me but now, what I am doing.

Just like that ...

"Jogi, that is why I want to liberate her and attain salvation yourself."

"I've seen an artist in you; the mainstream will indeed accept you. You want to be a celebrity, but you have to be prepared for it. Gilda Radner was a comedian. She had cancer.

She missed her alchemy date for one of her shows.

Charlie was deported from the United States. The artist is the one who challenges the establishment.

You, too, are the trust of the people.

I am not saying that you should leave Raman.

I am saying that you should release her. Make her understand how to lead a healthy life.

"Helen, I don't understand you completely. I just think that you want me ultimately. You are becoming possessive.

You want my man completely naked. You saw Raman in me.

"My dear, you are very innocent. Your Perspective on life is very naive and divisive. How old are you

"Thirty-Five Years"

"And Raman's?"

"She is three years younger."

"I mean, she's thirty-two years old. See, the path you are about to take is very broken. It will take at least fifteen years for people to get to know you and add twenty more to reach on TOP. I'm sure once you make history, you will grow old, but it will become a way to send a message to people and all this time, you have to stay in Canada; what will Raman do without you?

It will take time for your Bittu to complete his studies."

"So?"

Helen laughed and said, "The possessiveness of both of you will poison your life. Have you ever seen soldiers fighting from afar? They also come back but become mentally ill. The fire of the body burns everyone's woman or man. You say you love her. If this is true, then tell her the truth that you sleep with me. At the time of bed, I have realized that you have got used to me. Even in your sleep, your limbs are looking for their comfort zone.

Isn't it Raman's right to associate with anyone?"

When Jogi did not answer, Helen said, "Look, my son saw my need and introduced you to me so that my mother could have a happy moment." I also think that you have art, and he has music; your duo reached the top.

"But how can I tell her?"

"If you can't tell her on the phone, email her. It will be easy. If your alleged rituals do not allow you to do so, send her a picture of me and tell her that you sleep with this white woman? Whatever you choose from courage and deceit. My thinking is. Make her feelings so thin that she can live; she has the right to breathe."

Jogi picked up the phone and redialed India Raman's number.

"Hello"

"Yes, Raman, I had one thing to say. Nowadays, I am taking classes from a female friend."

"So, dear, what's the point?"

"Raman, I see a lot of flames in her; that Flame is even darker than you. Take care of Bittu."

Before Raman could answer, Jogi hung up.

CHOICE

S HE WAS A lawyer by profession in Albania. Low in English but carrying a degree and a license to advocate would be repeated again and again.

No matter what the issue was, she had to speak up, even if it always went off the rails. Dorthy, you should take English classes. Whenever groups were formed, I had to help her by taking all the steps to include her in my group. Whether she was questioned in the group now or not, she always wanted the most critical role. During the group discussion at Moot Court, she was also in our group, and we spent two weekends together in Kenny's office.

Pot Luck, it was easy for me; Punjabi samosas would have survived, and the chickpeas would have become home, and this dish would have been the best. Dorthy worked hard for Pot Luck and brought a bottle of vodka. I wrote the Moot-Court script, and everyone liked it. Now the writing was mine, and I had the right to present it, but this could not be agreed upon. In this way, I would have looted the whole show. There were six in our group, Dorthy, Kenny, Georgia, Binny, Vernon, and I. Three men and three women. Binny, Dorthy, and Varna were women. Binny was from Newfoundland, and Vern was Italian. Dorthy and I were both over-aged. We were both the same age. We all had to bow to Dorthy's insistence.

The whole class was supposed to be in this show, and the marks that the teacher had to give were the responsibility of the entire group. The same effects were to be delivered.

Dorthy was paying the price because my role was too much, so she did me too much favor. I was fully aware of her hypocrisy. I was annoyed when she tried to seduce with her Women's claims.

By the time she finished halfway through the paralegal, Dorthy was good in English. There was no problem while writing, but he had to emphasize while speaking. As I began to cross-examine the witness in the moot court, my questions broadly promoted our presentation. Dorthy was playing the judge's role, and the group also wrote her judgment; the group rejected her written conclusion. One of Dorthy's compliments is that she insisted but didn't get angry and accepted everything as if she realized her mistake.

"Dorthy, at this age, how did you come to Canada?" I asked on the way to Long Drive.

"Amar, it's hard to get out of Albania, no matter where you go next. Jimmy has a big hand in it. If he hadn't dared, I would have died there." I realized that the talk was long and that there was Nothing to do in the moving car.

"What kind of practice did you have there?"

"It wasn't about making money; it was about obeying Jimmy.

I made money at the level of the upper class, but still, the confidence of life was gone."

"Who is Jimmy, your husband, or someone else?"

"Husband ... no ... no ... but my everything. Twenty years have passed with Jimmy. Yes, Jimmy was married but lost romance with his wife, and they divorced. Until then, Jimmy's wife did not know why I was handling the case for free."

"Interesting; when did she find out?"

"No, Amar, the matter is not as easy as you think. She didn't even know what our relationship was until then."

"What was your relationship like, who filed for divorce free of charge?"

"We were just friends, just like you and me."

"Isn't it like I'm going to become Jimmy for you? have a baby?" I joked.

"Just forget Amar, you can't be Jimmy, you don't have that much talent, it can't be. You're just Amar, not Jimmy, and you're also married, you dummy!"

"And what if I get divorced?"

"Then you don't be a husband or a human just animal."

"Why?"

Honey doesn't even joke like that. God bless your family. Don't say that. Everyone has their destiny; these happenings are influential, just like a flower blooms in a particular season and its land. It dries up in another land."

"No, Dorthy, I was just kidding."

"I know you're kidding, you're just like Jimmy, but you're a man of a different land. My heartfelt wish is that someday I will meet you with Jimmy, but it is not possible. It is not feasible for me to meet him now."

"Why isn't it possible for you?"

"You don't know my country. It's not easy to get out.

Jimmy not at all, because he's in a wheelchair, he's paralyzed from the waist down, he was shot in the back, survived, but permanently disabled, but he's Crackbrained."

"What mean?"

"Amar, his disability is only physical; he still thinks positive. Very funny with me, always talk naughty on every subject."

"Talk about sex with you."?

"How do you know? Always, all the time. Your intuition is correct."

"Very simple," Amar replied.

"Exciting Amar. First time I feel Jimmy just sits beside me."

"Now, if the word 'Crackbrained' comes up, it can become a different image for both of us. I can say that Crackbrained is the one who does his own thing by listening to his mind."

Is your wife know about this?"

"so careless? Never ask"

"why"?

"She is living with crack; you dump Dorthy."

"I know, just kidding, my inner Jimmy is pushing me to ask these silly questions."

"Let's find another word for Jimmy," I asked.

"Too late, Amar. Now I can't think about this. I want him to go to Jesus Christ as soon as possible."

I fell silent; again, the problem was that it did not fall within the scope of the car seat.

On the way to Highway Four Hundred, Berry came to the outskirts. Ford's big signs began to appear. I intended to return from Berry, but I did not know about Dorthy yet. I took the exit, and now my eyes were looking for a coffee shop. We didn't have to go very far. Soon there was a coffee shop, and we parked our car and went inside. We took a coffee and sat in a corner. We were seated at the beginning of the highway so that it would be easy to return.

We were just sitting when my cell rang. "Hello, darling."

"That's you; what does my government do?" I asked romantically.

"Just what to do else, waiting for you."

"Don't worry, wait, waiting is more romantic than Reunion."

"Yes, you don't like our union now."

"No, it's not like that, darling. It's just like dialogue. I'll be back in two or three hours."

I hung up.

"Was it your wife's phone?" Dorthy asked.

"My girlfriend's."

"Do you have a girlfriend when you're married?"

"Can't a wife be a girlfriend?" I laughed.

"That U Rascal, your words are very deceptive, just like Jimmy's."

"No, Dorthy, words are just words, but there is deception in our psyche. Now it is as if you were deluded."

"No, it's my wife.

The girlfriend, the one who takes you beyond the clutter of the world. The phone call was from my girlfriend, not my wife."

Amar, why do I feel like you're trying to trap me?" Just by manipulating words." I thought in my heart that only a fool could try to seduce you.

"No, these are your criteria; I have no such intention. It seems like men and women worldwide think the same thing, I thought differently about you, but your thinking is the same as I think. Don't get me wrong. I'm not used to eating grass anyway."

"You're naughty, don't say that; I'm not grass." Maybe you have no idea; only Jimmy knows what I am?"

"Looks like you forgot the life art class; you know what Jenny was saying?"

Jenny came to our class to lecture on life art. she said In her introduction, "You learn a lot from experiences.

Sometimes these experiences are not your own, but whoever has them must have a message that reaches you like someone else. In other words, we can say that you have some end of your thinking. The myths of cultures around the world are so full of tales that even myths become an excuse to create something new."

"I agree with Jenny," Dorthy said. Without telling the truth, what she said was written in my heart; in fact, it is Jimmy's philosophy." I could see that she would inadvertently involve Jimmy in everything. Jimmy was on guard at every turn.

About four months ago, I was attending a class. I was the only Punjabi in the course of 26 persons. The theme was "How to Get Success in Real Life." Jenny, the teacher in this class, was about sixty years old. She was a nurse by profession.

When the health services decided to adopt a new system to cut their costs, Jenny did not like it and quit.

She enrolled in social studies and successfully got a job in social services. Determined, soon began giving the group lectures.

"She asked a question in class, have any of you ever been bored, or at some point in the day.

Why didn't you raise your hand, Dorthy?"

"I saw you raise your hand. So I kept quiet."

I was the only one in the whole class who raised his hand, surrendered, and asked what the cure for not getting bored was.

First of all, Jenny said, "It's too bad if you're bored at any moment. Does that mean you don't know how to live?" Before I could speak, Jenny spoke again, "If you can't make your life interesting on your own, what else can you do for society?"

"I knew Dorthy this truth was not mine alone. Twenty-five of the twenty-six people in this class is not as healthy as Jenny wants them to be. I became a target by talking. Some friendly people were smiling as if teasing me; others were messing around. Many of them were bored and made others bored, even in the three-hour class."

"Absolutely."

"Anyone can be bored to hear what Jenny said later, but if you want to know the gist, it can be said that Jenny's lecture had a significant impact on the whole class. Many reasons cannot be understood for free, so either you have to listen to a study or read the experiences closely.

As I am listening to you about Jimmy."

"I feel good to hear that you want to know about Jimmy. The big deal is that you need to find the cause of the stress and increase the engagement to have no free time left in the moment of boredom. Still, your engagements should be as interesting as you like, even if these are sudoku? Why not the desire to enter the lottery and check?"

"Come on, Dorthy, why not looking for the moment you with Jimmy in the bed. Tell me a little bit about yourself, how this beautiful Albanian girl came to Canada as a parcel to bore us."

"Amar, aren't you sick?" Any mental illness?"

"Why do you think I'm sick? Good to hear so I don't have to scare now. My wife always advises me don't let anybody rape me."

"What dangers are you afraid of, Amar?" This aspect of Dorthy I never thought possible. She was also severe in her jokes. It was time to turn things around.

"Jenny said that running away and getting out of the situation doesn't work; that's what makes you bored. Ask yourself, what is your choice? Accept the challenge if you can. Even if you can't, don't be in the middle. Staying in the middle creates stress that leads to boredom. Make sure you are allowed. You have the right to be with yourself; you can't run away from it." I quoted Jenny.

"Yes, Amar, I remember Jenny's words. But you don't know anything about Jimmy. I'll tell you, then maybe you'll understand me better."

"No, Dorthy, I've learned from my experience that you don't believe in escaping."

"I am on the run, from my country.

Never to return, but this flee of mine is not going to run away on its own."

I fell silent. My silence is saying something to Dorthy I want to know about you. My lust has brought me to Long Drive. I often derail just to get the hang of it.

Dorthy broke the silence and asked me to bring another cup of coffee.

"I had a restaurant near my law school with Jimmy as the manager," Dorthy said as she sipped her coffee.

In our free time, we used to come to this restaurant and spend a lot. Sometimes Jimmy would be included in our consummingy. At times, we even thought we'd spend less money, more time at the restaurant, but Jimmy never complained. He would instead encourage us. In return, we would order more. Also, they praised the restaurant to Other students so that Jimmy's subscription could increase.

I don't know when I started thinking about Jimmy.

As I slept through the night, Jimmy's presence would be revealed to me. His smiling face insisted on sleeping with me, and I would get the idea of his existence with me and go to sleep warmly. As soon as I woke up in the morning, filled with some desire, coming to my heart, today I will see Jimmy again. Facing Jimmy, an invitation would stick to my face. Jimmy felt the invitation on my face."

"How old were you, Dorthy?"

"That's about twenty-two years."

"At this age, invitations are not issued but are flown in the air."

"No, I had already seen it, flying in the air. No one asks for flying leaves. I became serious even at that age. Only attached leaves to trees can prevent dust. The whole tree protects a single leaf, but the broken and dancing leaf has only its personality, and dust is extreme. Stray in the air makes the leaf useless. My eyes were also ashamed before the dust. I was waiting to be reunited with the tree."

"And Jimmy?"

"He was in no hurry. He was not feeling my intensity at all. He thought that I was Adolescence. Nothing else; he was not trying to understand my feelings. Sometimes I think he understands everything but pretends not to understand."

"Maybe Jimmy doesn't even look at you that way."

"Amar, that was it. He was married, and I did not know it yet. One day there was a big storm. At that time, I was alone in the restaurant. It was raining outside, and I could not get out. Jimmy was worried about me. He made several attempts, but no attempt was successful, then he started talking to me to divert my attention. Restaurant employees had also stopped work. It was Jimmy's responsibility to get everyone home; that's when I found out. It was not part of his job as a manager, but he considered it his duty. Two hours after the restaurant closed, Jimmy asked the chef to prepare food for everyone, and he was always thinking.

Just when the whole market was numb, a cab stopped in front of the restaurant. Jimmy went out and talked to him, and he looked happy when he returned. The cab driver ate the food as well. All the employees were taken to their respective homes in groups. I was deliberately late, so I could spend some more time with Jimmy. It was my turn, and as I began to walk, I grabbed Jimmy's hand. My grabbing was an open invitation to Jimmy. Still, Jimmy turned a blind eye to that invitation and smiled and said good-bye."

"It was a golden opportunity for Jimmy." I laughed.

"Yes, it was golden, but only gold, but gold also does not have fragrance. Immortality is only shone, and Jimmy did not know how to trade glitter."

"Very noble person."

"Don't tell him noble, Jimmy was very naughty, I found out later, but we both had to pay a lot of prices. Where could we find love without the price?"

"No, Dorthy, it's not a cheap deal, so what happened?"

"It only came to my notice then. Jimmy never hurt anybody. He was not with his wife from the heart.

He was pretending everything. His wife could not get Jimmy from the heart. I never knew why his wife did not reach the depth of what supposed to be. How come anybody ignores Jimmy. Only his wife had that bad luck. Jimmy was there in a show-room. His wife never took him out from the show-room.

The living person could not stay forever in the show-room. Jimmy wanted to come out, but he was just tired, but he didn't give up his choice, and it wasn't in his mind.

One day sitting next to me, his eyes filled with tears. It was a choice for Jimmy to go out or go in, but he couldn't decide, and the tears dried in his eyes."

"So nice, Dorthy, you make me think a bit deep. Now I could feel the boy inside me too and dry tears."

"Dorthy, do you know how marriage works?"

"No," Dorthy said curiously.

"Once this relationship is formed, both of them want to be one with the soul.

Can't be, and then the choice comes to break the relationship or break it and live, the thoughts of both human beings can never be the same."

"Amar, that's the way it is, and that's what happened to Jimmy, but his fate is not in the drama, and he decided with his wife. The wife did not know the reason, but she could not bear the boredom and decided to get a divorce by mutual consent. By then, Jimmy hadn't paid any attention to me, but his eyes started shining after that, which I could read. I was already dedicated, and he, too, took me in his arms on a beautiful day. I took all Jimmy inside me."

My God, what did you do?" I said with a laugh.

"You're a naughty boy!"

"Let's go back to Toronto; the rest is fine." I was in a hurry to return after three hours.

"No, not yet. My story has just begun. I will not let you go without telling you."

"Your story doesn't end all night, and you don't have anybody. No body waiting for you. But somebody is waiting for me at home, and anyway, I'm in a romantic mood today; I want someone to wrap me up today, let me go now."

"No, sir, not today."

"Okay, let's go. I'll call home to tell that Jimmy is busy today, somewhere else."

Don't dream, and listen carefully to what I have to say, and your knowledge will increase."

I motioned for Dorthy to shut up and started calling.

"Yes, what does my government do?"

"Waiting"

"Don't wait; I may not be able to come home today; I came to New Market to meet my client, and now the car is not starting. I don't know if the starter is faulty or a chip has been shaken. Nine o clock now, there is no mechanic at this time. I have to wait till morning."

"Oh God, what happened? You didn't even take your medicine with you. How many times I told you always to keep your medicine in the car, but you never listen. what will you do now?"

"What to do, God is everything. I will sleep in the car."

"No, don't sleep in the car; there is no motel nearby?" If you say so, I will come with my brother. You eat something or not?"

"No, there's no need to come; it'll not be good to ask your brother in the middle of the night."

"No, I am coming; we will pick up the car tomorrow."

"Why don't you understand? I am not a child. I am tired of your overprotection, don't worry too much and go to sleep comfortably. I will get up in the morning, fix the car, and reach by noon."

"Well, why are you angry? I said the same thing. I have nowhere to sleep now, you are in the desert, and I go to sleep, in peace. How can that be?"

"Well, then do it like this, take a sleeping pill and sleep. You have to go to work in the morning."

"Well, as you say, take care. Go to the motel and get some sleep. Don't let your blood sugar increase by starving."

"Nothing happens overnight. Good night."

"Good night, may God have mercy on you."

"Good night, sweetheart." I hung up and breathed a sigh of relief.

"It's nice to listen to a long conversation between you and your wife. It's comforting to know that there are happy people in the world." Dorthy spoke in the car.

"Where are we going now, Dorthy?"

"Orillia is said to be a great place and a nice ride on Highway Ninety."

"Have you already visit or read on Google?"

"I came here once with a friend. He was very bored; he was not like you."

"Very nice views are there but what to see at night, but if you say so, we can take another hour-long drive."

"Yes, Amar, I say, turn to Orillia. At night we will talk by the lake. We'll be back in the morning with the first ray."

"Yes, as you say. Today's cost is on your head; I pay for gas."

"You are very mean. I've heard that men start by buying something."

"How do you know I'm a man? I did not agree to buy anything."

"Then give your consent to a woman and buy what I need; who stopped you?"."

"Look, don't talk so much if I have to spend; my answer is no. I don't have money."

"You mean man, then let's go back. You can't go home. Now you have to stop somewhere to sleep. I will give you a company, or I will phone your wife and tell her your husband is not listening to a helpless woman."

"Don't blackmail me. Let's make a deal. Everything fifty-fifty."

Dorthy pulled out a notebook and said, "Come on, tell me how much you pay for coffee?"

"Forget the coffee money; it is free from me, just write sixty dollars for gas."

"This is your car; why I pay anything for gas? not fair. I pay half only for coffee."

My thoughts turned to the first ray of the morning; of course, I have to get back with the first ray.

"From now until the first rays of the morning, everything is half over."

"I will never wake up in the morning; we will go back in the afternoon."

"You don't know my wife. Suppose I would not show up by ten. She will start looking for me and would find me in your arms."

"Who told you that, daydreamer?

"Dorthy, Sometimes you don't mean anything, but you still take care of the routine; how helpless a person becomes in the face of convention.

"If you don't wake up, I will make you wake up in the morning.

"Okay, dear, when you say, we'll leave early morning, but where to go now?"

Routinely, I said, "No matter where you go, you ruined my romantic night with my wife."

"Nowhere does it make a difference overnight? Sometimes it should be empty Stomach."

"Yes, that's fine too." As soon as we got out of the berry, we grabbed some food and a bottle of vodka.

"Dorthy, don't you drink too much vodka?" It is not the case with women in particular?".

"Do you think I'm an alcoholic?"

"Yes, Dorthy, take care of your health."

"I know, but Jimmy also drinks vodka. If he doesn't drink, he will die. The pain of his back will kill him." I also have to drink to support myself."

"But Jimmy isn't here anymore. Can you leave comfortably?"

"How come you don't know Jimmy?" He and my veins are mixed. I'm in danger of losing it."

"There's no danger, Dorthy; it's just a sign of danger that we're afraid. It's the fear that makes us feel bored; I remember Jenny talking about it."

When we reached Orillia, we parked our car in a parking lot by the lake and walked to the lake. It was hot all summer, but it was cold this time.

At Dorthy's urging, I grabbed a glass of vodka, and we felt warm.

Emptying the glass, Dorthy said, "My friend Jimmy is such a positive person that I can say that I have never met such a person. He is always in the rising art, still has something encouraging, and it is a heap of right words. If one of his employees is in a bad mood or has a bad day, Jimmy always helps him, and in the end, he says to look for the good in him.

Jimmy's behavior was going to amaze me; I would like to take him in my arms. One day I asked him, "Jimmy, how are you in a good mood all the time? How is that possible?"

Jimmy replied, "Look, every morning, I tell myself I have two choices for this day — whether I'm in a good mood or I'm in a bad mood. I always choose a good mood. When something bad happens, I have two choices: either I get sad or get angry or learn something from it. I choose to learn something new. That is how I choose to live my life."

I said, "Jimmy, it's not that easy."

"Yes, it's not that easy, but life is all about choices," said Jimmy. You can choose how people or circumstances can affect your mood, your life."

"One morning, Jimmy forgot to close the back door of the restaurant, and through the back door, three robbers armed with pistols entered the restaurant. According to their instructions, Jimmy tried to open the safe. Still, his hands were shaking due to nervousness. He forgot the numbers to open the safe, and the robbers shot him. Fortunately, help arrived on the scene, and Jimmy was rushed to the hospital. After several hours of surgery and deep care, Jimmy survived and was sent home."

I asked, "What was going on in his mind when the robbers were standing on his head?"

"I thought I should close the back door of the restaurant, and when I was bleeding, I remembered my choice; what should I do in this case?" Should I die or should I struggle to live?"

I asked, "Jimmy, were you scared then?"

"I was scared when they took me to the emergency room on a stretcher; I knew I had to do something," said Jimmy. When the nurse asked me if I was allergic to anything, I replied, "I'm allergic." The doctors and nurses immediately stopped working and became curious about my allergies. I took a deep breath and said I was allergic to bullets."

They all started laughing, and I said, "I have a strong desire to live. Do your job as I live, not to act as if I don't know if I want to live or die."

"What a Great Philosophy!" I said in a wave.

"My Jimmy is alive now. Of course, he is disabled. He lives only because of doctors' skill, and it happened because it is his nature to live; it is his nature that saved him. I learned from Jimmy that we should wish to live every day no matter what."

"A vibrant human being is your Jimmy. Did his disability make any difference?"

"No, not at all. The bullet hit the spinal cord, so Jimmy stopped walking and standing, but he found ways to live his life. The bullet of the robbers could not change his nature, his lively heart."

The cold wind shook me, and I saw that Dorthy was also shivering. I said, "Let's get in the car; now the wind is enjoying us."

Dorthy laughed and said, "Let's get in the car." We got in the car, and I took a sip of vodka, looked at Dorthy, she filled her glass too.

"Why don't we go to a motel? We can't live here anymore; our legs are starting to ache. Now it seems as if Jimmy's pain has come to me; he was always relieved in the cold. Whenever I started massaging him in such a situation, he would refuse and say no, this is how I will get used to it. I will be even more crippled."

I don't know what Dorthy was thinking, but there was a clear need for her.

She put a double peg of vodka and drank it in one gulp.

I could observe her state of mind.

Dorthy said, "Today I want to talk openly with you about Jimmy, let's get him involved, and then in a minute, she started crying drunk."

I didn't say anything, thinking that silencing it wouldn't make it go away.

"You know Amar; I am terrified of good people; I do not feel comfortable in their company. I like the company of those who talk nonsense."

"Why is that, Dorthy?"

"Maybe in Jimmy's absence, I want to avoid him. I don't want to listen to good people."

"Dorthy, I think you are mixing wise and good words."

"Yes, you are right. Jimmy delivered good words, and he is the right person too.

He would crawl into bed and then start screaming, but positivity never disappeared even at that time. And whenever he did, he would say,

"Dorthy, you know what do I want?"

"No"

"I know, Dorthy, your answer would be no."

"Then Amar, I can't speak anymore because I knew all his answers. All he had to say was, 'I don't want to be yelled at; I want to live with normal breathing.' My silence would not reassure him, and he would say what I had already thought."

Dorthy closed her eyes and keep mum.

These things were new to me but not superficial, I think I should have known, but now I know that I think the same way. Where does Raman make me feel? I do not know?

Dorthy's silence didn't need any response from me.

"Amar, these were the days when I began to feel an unknown fear. There was a silence between us."

"I was scared of his choice. You have to be afraid of someone who has been thinking all his life positively and also loves you unconditionally.

"Dorthy's tongue began to tremble, but she drank another peg to control her tongue.

For a moment, her voice recovered, and in that voice, she said, "Let's go to a motel and relax."

I hadn't even backed the car yet, and she insisted that she will drive.

Saying no to a drunken person means making even more stubborn, even though it was dangerous. Still, I handed the car over to her. She carefully backed the car and got back on Highway Ninety. I knew there was an exit at two kilometers, so I cleverly told her that there was a motel next to the exit, so take the exit.

She took the exit with confidence, but there was no motel. There was a local road, and I wanted her to take the local road. The intoxication, the strong wind blowing on the highway, would bring her even closer to Jimmy. There could be no talking on the road, so her loneliness would get Jimmy inside the car, and my life could have been lost in an accident.

By the way, the day was good, and we had just gone a little further when the Super Eight Motel appeared. Thankfully, I also have a problem that alcohol doesn't affect me in danger. Still, as soon as I stood in the parking lot of the motel, my lost intoxication returned.

As we entered the room, Dorthy looked at the vodka bottle as if reassured that night would pass. The bottle was still half full, but I didn't know if it was enough for Dorthy.

"Can you get more vodka from this motel?" Her question was right, just like I thought, "We have to find out, by the way, this facility is not available in Super Eight. Go and find out if you can find it."

The manager of Super Eight was Punjabi Bai.

I asked, he said no from the motel, but I have my scotch, take it. I paid for the cost. I tried to give him more. He said, don't worry; you don't have to pay extra.

When I entered the room, Dorthy was reclining in her chair as if she were ill.

"That's how Jimmy used to sit."

"He's forced, but you?"

"I like sitting like that."

"Will you eat?"

"No"

"Why?"

"Even Jimmy didn't eat when he was drunk."

I thought it would be just a matter of Jimmy today; I am not Jimmy.

"What were you talking about on the shores of the lake?" I asked.

"Jimmy was getting weaker day by day, and sometimes he would get upset with me, and then he would get better on his own. Maybe he thought that there was no solution to his problem, and I am not going to get rid of him."

"Sit well, today is heartbreaking; let me tell you a lot about Jimmy."

"Do it, just to hear what you have to say, and I lied at home just for you."

"But you shouldn't have lied, Amar." If your wife loves you, she can understand everything you say."

"Dorthy, I don't think she needs it. I know she programmed to hear lies."

"Have you ever tried? Maybe she'll understand; why can't you be a jimmy?"

"Come on; it's not that easy."

"First I had to get up, Tonight I will become Jimmy's bride, and then Dorthy swallowed a bottle of vodka."

I went to the washroom too, and when I came back, Dorthy said, "Do you understand my fear?"

"Yes, I understand, but you tell me."

"What do you understand?"

"That's all there is to it, Jimmy's choice."

"Yeah, Al, that sounds pretty crap to me.

"You cannot guess about Jimmy. Not even about his sex.

He is lame but still a man of men."

I laughed and said, "Let me try."

"Become a jimmy and do whatever you want."

"No, Dorthy, this is your trip. Come on, do your things; what were you going to say about positivity."

"It was a night, furious. Jimmy, a daily drinker, was in pain but was not drinking. In fact, in the evening, a pain wire would rise in his spinal cord, which filled his whole body with pain. According to our finances, we saw many doctors. Still, it was not a disease of the average doctor, and a specialist's cost was high. Jimmy could get treatment if he sold his two cabs. But he had the ghost of buying more cabs. At that time, he had ten cabs, and his pockets were full every evening. He and I would just sit on the dispatch. He used to work in a wheelchair. This fatigue would be so severe by evening that the spinal cord would wake up and bother him.

He had to drink alcohol to escape from pain and have some sleep, and he also drank until he fainted."

"Was your Jimmy working under the influence of alcohol? Was that his choice?" I sighed.

"Yeah, Al, that sounds pretty crap to me. You cannot understand until you listen completely and with all your concentration. People like you have a habit of biting."

The bell rang outside for so long. There was a pizza delivery. I started taking pizza delivery, and Dorthy went to the balcony and started smoking.

"And then what happened next?"

"If you want to listen, don't interrupt and don't comment anything in between. First, listen, and then you have all the right to comment."

"If not, I'll tell you. Your interruption breaks my wire. Anyway, everyone thinks according to their logic." I was embarrassed to hear Dorothy."

"Let's not interrupt now; I'll talk to you later." I still defended myself.

"Only when he was asleep would I get up and go to bed and sleep. He was in pain that day but refused to drink. I kept asking her to drink. He had made a decision today and wanted to let me know." My curiosity was growing.

"Dorothy, you know me well, yes or no." Jimmy began to say.

"Do you have any doubts about that?"

"No doubt, but I have never done such a thing to you before. You know that whenever I have two directions in front of me, I always choose a positive direction."

"King, that is why I am your slave."

"No, no, no, you are my life, that's why time is passing; what I want to do is getting ahead, and now it's time for me to make my own choice."

Jimmy, realizing that he could no longer play the role, said, "I want you to leave Albania. That's all." We are well off."

"But how can I leave you?" That is not possible."

"Why is it not possible when I have decided."

Dorothy fell silent. She needed Jimmy to speak, and she emptied her glass to capture the moment.

"Jimmy was sure of the tune once he decided, his hand wasn't hidden from me, but Jimmy couldn't be so hard, so he played politics with me and said," I am not doing this for you alone. I am doing it for both of us. Look, we can't get out of Albania together, first, you get out, then there will be a struggle for me to get out."

"But Jimmy, you know how risky it is to die. Will you tolerate my death?"

I got up from my seat, walked around the room to open my legs, and then sat down.

"Jimmy acted to make it clear and said, 'Can't you sacrifice so much for me now?'

"That's just Jimmy's prank so that I can hear the next thing?"

Dorthy paused for a moment, then closed her eyes and spread her legs on the table. My gaze slipped from her closed eyes, from her thighs to her legs. She was wearing a transparent nightie, and my longing thanked her with her closed eyes. She was thinking about something else, and I started thinking about something else. As if I didn't have much time, she could open her eyes at any time, and I was taking full advantage of the time in between.

She spoke as if she were talking to me with her eyes closed, but she was proud of Jimmy. "In those days, people had to flee by boat. In the dark of night, people would take risks, many would-be killed, and many would survive. How could Jimmy put me in such great danger? I was convinced that Jimmy must have found another way. In which there is no fear of life.

I asked Jimmy, and he said, "Dorthy, today I kept two cabs and sold the whole fleet. Immediately handed over to minister's P. A. He has taken the money and said yes."

"But Jimmy, this is a big gamble, what if he refuses later?"

"Then I will shoot him, but I know he will not die. I have given him your passport and also got a journalist license for you. You have to take your job letter from the Herald newspaper and give it to him, and he will do it himself. He will include you in the official delegation to Germany, and you will reach Germany. Albanians have an extradition treaty with Germany, so you don't have to stop there. I have arranged to send you to Canada. Once in Canada, you have to apply for refugee status. Canada considers Albanians to be bonafide refugees.

When you get immigration, you could apply for me on a marriage basis. We will get married, and then we go for a honeymoon." Jimmy laughed out loud.

"Then what happened?" I said, looking at Dorothy in silence.

Dorothy burst into tears and cried, "Jimmy cheated on me. He spent his entire fleet and sent me to Canada, but he refused to come."

"Why?"

"I call every day. He refused to come and said that we would never meet again; my life is short. He had an infection in her spinal cord, but he didn't tell me when I was in Albania. Treatment was possible, but expensive. He had a choice, get his treatment, or expel me from Albania. He made the second choice. The infection causes pain, and there is no immediate risk. He is continually taking antibiotics, but the infection is spreading slowly in the body; it is not sure when his organs will be covered entirely, but life is only three to five years.

Two years have passed so far. I try to keep him happy. I call every day. He is delighted and even mischievously talks about that I will neither die nor live. Jimmy is very fond of sex. He is addicted to oral sex. I'm too tired to pretend; how many fabrications can be told now?"

We went to bed at four in the morning. It was one o'clock in the afternoon when I woke up. Oh my God, so long ... at home, my wife must be sad. I tried turning on my closed cell. There were six phone calls. The two phones belonged to my brother-in-law. They must be looking for me, oh my god, what should I do now? How do I tell where the night has been so far? Now only a car breakdown could have saved me, but what excuse would I give not to call? It's a lot of trouble for me now.

I was driving on Highway Ninety. Dorthy was sitting next to me. She looked a little fresh, and after drinking coffee on the way, she started chirping and said, "Why are you so quiet? You used to jump a lot at night, and I didn't even feel fat then."

"I used to jump; you were not with me but with Jimmy. I was just a second man."

"Yes, that's right, Amar. What can I do? As long as no one becomes Jimmy, I can't become a woman." Healed, you too become Jimmy. I'll tell Jimmy tonight; it's all over happenings."

"Watt ... will you tell all this to Jimmy?"

"He would be happy to listen, and I came to Long Drive with you. Can't you tell your wife?"

"The question does not arise."

"How long has your marriage been?"

"That's about twenty-two years."

"You haven't learned to share your happiness with anyone in so long?"

-No--

--- What's the problem? -

"Just never wondered what the problem is."

"Isn't it okay to go with me?"

"No"

"Then, why did you go?"

"Just like that ..."

"In two choices, one has to choose between falsehood and truth, but everyone has to make a choice, whether they live for themselves or someone else, but they have to make a decision.

Life without a choice is incomplete a big fraud.

I kept quiet and kept avoiding speeding cars on the highway, pretending that my focus was driving.

SPARROW

I WAS DELIGHTED WITH my husband Kulwant, daughter Daman and son Narangi. Sparrow Jani joined our family and became part of the family. She was a darling of Daman, and she would stay with her. Then our family was spotted, and everything fell apart. Johnny also left, but before leaving, I was taught the way of life.

Those were the days when Jani, taking advantage of the open cage, had fluttered her wings and flown away. A calamity had befallen the house. Daman's entire routine was tied to Jani. Everyone entering the house always talked to Jani first of all. Many of the complaints and grouses were settled through Jani. Instead of saying anything directly, Kulwant would convey his messages to others through Jani, especially what would happen on Friday, even Jani had begun to guess. I feel Jani had developed a foreknowledge of weeks and days. She would start to feel very happy right from the dawn of Friday and go on dancing and hopping without even a hyper tablet. However, Kulwant had to come in the evening with all his pretense. I remember even today when I told Kulwant for the first time,

"What are you doing? Have some sense of shame. Jani is looking at us."

And Kulwant had torn himself away from me and felt ashamed. After that, Kulwant had never done such frivolity in front of Jani; it seemed to me as if Jani was teasing us. She was not only Daman's friend but mine

49

too. I liked her special day and particular behavior very much. Everything, including Daman's happiness, the house's glory, the correctness thereof, had been jeopardized. People could say anything about this. Leaving the house by the sparrow had become something to be laughed at. It was a bad omen in away. The entire routine of the house had changed. Right from Kulwant to Narangi, anybody entering the house talked to Jani first of all. For everything, Jani's nod was sought. The empty cage scared us much.

Today I got a headache again and took two pills of Advil. I was trying to sleep, then the phone rings.

I stared at the ringing phone that seemed to have eyes staring back at me.

Finally, I picked up the phone.

"Hello," I said, looking at my watch, showing 11 PM.

"Hello, Dear," the voice oozed out of the phone and sat just by my pillow.

I got irritated. Had I kept my specs in my reach, recognizing the number, I wouldn't have picked up the receiver.

"I phoned last night too. Were you out somewhere?"

Resham's artificially soft voice sounded relatively coarse to me.

"Yesterday I was not feeling well, brother. I was asleep after taking a pill."

"O, that's all right. I thought you were gone somewhere."

I understood the dual meaning of what Resham had said, but I didn't say anything.

"Look, never think that you are all alone. We can stand by through thicks and thins, and we will face all this together. Has Kulwant come to know about Master Rana?"

"I respect you a lot, brother. Not because you are from my village, but you are Kulwant's fast friend. What is this you have touched upon at mid-night? Did you ever phoned like this in Kulwant's presence?" I tried to bury my anger under the weight of my restraint.

"No, no, I mean Kulwant is not a wrong person. He is very responsible, though he behaves boyish sometimes. But who is Mr. Clean here?

Don't fill in Master Rana's immigration papers when we are here."

"Please, brother, hang up the phone now. My children are around.

50

And you shouldn't ring anyone when you are drunk. Lest I should say something unpleasant," I flared up a bit.

"Now, your rage is for nothing. Am I a stranger? I belong to your village.

"All right. Sat Sri Akal." I hung up.

I thought, 'Why would I explain this rascal? Who is he to poke in any of my affairs?

Last Sunday my car got punctured. Resham came with his wife. To be my bad luck and Resham's eyesore, Janardan also popped up to hand over the car key after having the puncture galvanized.

And Janardan too was such a bird who couldn't think of taking a flight. Reading what Resham had to say through his eyes, finally, I had to say that:

"Okay, Mr. Janardan, you might be getting late. Thanks a lot for getting the tire fixed."

I was thinking of Womankind, a mentality which is having an extensive history of its own. This history starts even before a woman takes birth. I would rather say that this history of a woman does not take delivery because one who dies is born again?

It is in their mind that a woman who is alone could be swallowed. I was not even divorced yet, but the people around me started putting ropes on me.

Last Saturday, Resham phoned and said

"If Janardan is with you, send him somewhere else. We are coming." I was stunned.

Who are these barons to mediate? They think they are blessed with wisdom. --Ha-- wise ones? They are just the butchers I want to throw out in the trash. But what could I do? They say that a drowning person catches at a straw. Janardan got me a narrow escape. If there is no compromise, let it be so. Who are you, by the way--The Brides Dad?

'I think a woman is another name of modesty. But modesty is not a trap.'

My hemicrania has changed. Now either I have ache all over my head or not at all. I had tried many remedies. I had cried quite a lot, as much as I could, even more than that. And then I began to hate my crying. After all, I was no longer a girl. Crying does not behoove a mother. A dread caravan came to fear me more.

Resham, The brother, head of this caravan, came to counsel me between right and wrong that I should patch up.

"With whom? My husband or you?"

Estranged eyes on some acquainted faces seemed to say, "If you don't compromise, we will kick you out from society.

No crematorium does cremate this fear. And who is Janardan, after all? He, too, is a crematorium, but without fire.

I know my head has been bared. And for them, it is just a window that has opened with a bang. I have now begun to understand the complete history of the ladies' scarf on the head. When Kulwant stood with me like a rock, this Resham used to call me his sister. All are not alike. I know that. There are some in this advisory crowd -like father —It seems to me that they have not come to counsel, but just to play with me. Can the broken families be happy this way?

People like Resham are building bubbles of water in their minds, filling in the bubbles the colors of their choice, and then getting lost in this colorful world. What will your children do? "What your bubbles have to do with my children?" I wish I could ask.

Many of those who barely know anything about the issue were counseling me.

This is what I had told Daman and my elder son, as well. But neither they have the maturity, nor they have the capability. Instead of being cruel, I am adopting another path shown to me by Jani, a sparrow., what these sagacious people are unable to understand. But why are they to blame? They do not know about any sparrows. Even I did not know what was in her mind till the time of her leaving the house.

After sending off the so-called advisers, I shut the door and heaved a sigh of relief. I did not get into any of the cages brought by them.

I love him very much, even today. Every pour on my body is indebted to him. He was my sustenance, a very hard working person with a robust body. He could face the might of the mountains.

Like Ferhad, he could dig a canal of milk. He was an enterprising person. He had spared no effort. He had never counted the hours in a day. The roof above me has been given to me by my master. How does it matter if I have to seek shelter with the law? He had never given in during the legal battle. He had kept his courage intact. The count of his working hours also remained unchanged. I cried bitterly, begging him to own my daughter and to forgive my son. He could receive the price, therefore, from me. He could give me a few more blows on my body.

When my tears had dried, I heard my inner voice first of all. Who is he to forgive my elder son? Which is the society he is talking about? Can't I, his wife, along with her children, have a place in his social circle? For how long could I have tolerated all this? Is my sacrifice not good enough? Who is faithless, that aberrant rascal, or me? Why should we talk about this shop for faithlessness? Are we parents now? The serpents of the past had died long back; even the hide cast by them has dried and gone stiff. I just learned a lesson.

I got a divine word through a bird.

Daman had spent many evenings teaching the bird, "My name is Jani, my name is Jani." We would laugh until we have abs fatigue.

"It is not a parrot; my daughter and the sparrows can't talk. They can only chirp. You can know from their chirping whether they are thirsty, hungry, sad, or happy."

What a great truth Kuwait was telling! He explained one or the other meaning of this explanation or that meaning that I could understand had its root been very deep down in the earth. I was wondering whether Kulwant had an idea of the importance of those words at all? Perhaps not-Men-Kulwant's way of thinking is not the same, which I, a woman—a mother, could have. I had chirped too—a silent-chirping—which no one could understand, except, of course, my mother.

"Change the tone of your chirping, my daughter." And I changed at once as I had no time to lose? The freeze of the food was broken, and I filled the pot of my share.

When Daman was born, my elder son's birthday had just passed. The gap between them doesn't matter. It could be from a month to a year. It's just a matter of feeling. If I were exaggerating, I could say that for Kulwant, this gap maybe years, and me a few minutes. Kulwant was thrilled. He wanted a daughter. The birth of our daughter was celebrated in a big way. Everyone was saying, "How good are these progressive people of the modern age.

"Do you know that a house without a daughter lacks delicacy, mannerism, high values, etiquette, and daintiness," Kulwant asserted? He believed in this. The master of the house, as he was, had really made his daughter a decoration piece. – a sparrow with colorful feathers in a cage dangling amidst the living room. The intricacy of this sparrow appealed to the guests. Our taste impressed all of them. Kulwant strived to maintain the splendor of the house. I simply destroyed his wooden castle in which he put his blood and sweat. And that God-fearing had not objected to it at all.

Any claims my lawyer put across were acceptable to him. And for all the relatives, it was me to blame. It was me to muck. I, too, was holding myself blameworthy. Before breaking the relationship, before locking the cage for the last time, I had done my best to keep family together in my way. I had deprived the family's head, even of the rights due to him for over a year, but it had made no difference.

Was I happy making all they claim? Was I doing this for myself? I was just drinking this poison for the sake of my children. I was even claiming Kulwant. He can call us even today, provided there is warmth in his call. Let him become a dad and give all the rightful joys to his daughter Daman. After separation, he sent a new car to Daman. Dad could provide all comforts and facilities to his daughter, but not Peter. I don't insist on the elder son. It's all between son and father, all that I can say. Even I do not want the elder son should come back. He should be happy wherever he is, rather than live in daily turmoil. With whom I am concerned most is Daman. How long would this dominance continue, after all? It would have to be stopped sooner or later.

"Papa, I do not know. I never asked him his last name." Daman had stood before him with tears in her eyes that day."

"You do not know, but everybody in the world knows the creed of that son of a…dog. We are Jat-Sardars. We even do not eat if they are around."

"Why don't you talk with ease? Heavens have not fallen. You too are…"

"What can be a greater fall? I would suggest this matter is left here by both of you, a mother-daughter duo, lest I should have to cut you to pieces and throw you off in the lake. I have broken my back toiling hard day and night, and when the time has come for me to lead a respectable life, you have done this to bring a bad name to me."

Daman's father, who had ever been eager to do anything to fulfill even her minor wishes to please her, was so furious.

"Don't worry, Papa. I won't do anything which would hurt my sweet dad in any way." Daman had said this after looking at me. She had loved Kulwant deeply from the very beginning. She called him Papa or Dad affectionately. The same way she called Jani jinni when she had to show her greater love for her.

When Jani left the house, One of Kulwant's friends had said, "Perhaps you were starving her."

Another one went a step further and adduced another reason before us, "What could the poor thing do being all alone?"

Afraid of such pin-pricks, Kulwant wanted to get a substitute for Jani as soon as possible. Before the people came to know of this, he wanted to bring a new sparrow in the dangling cage. Also, he could not bear his daughter's anguish. As directed by Kulwant, I reached the pet shop with the three children of mine.

"You should go for yourself. She does not listen to me."

She did not want to go. With great difficulty had I led her towards the car.

"Let's go. I will see it."

I said a bit sternly to my elder son. Coming out of the pet shop, I said, "What a pity! What will happen to this girl? Did I let the sparrow fly? Is my pain in any way less than hers?

"Narangi was absorbed in watching the little colorful fish frolicking in the water. I stopped for a moment. Narangi turned his eyes a little to gaze at me, and again it busied himself in watching the fish. I came out of the shop. Daman was sitting on the bench opposite the footlocker. Going towards the bench, I was looking sharply at Daman.

"It was not my daughter that I was looking at, but it was a girl. A strange thought had begun to stir in some capillary of my head. When do the daughters grow up, one has no idea? I beckoned to my daughter Daman. She ignored me. It appeared to me as if Daman, my daughter, wanted to get up, but the girl's feet within her were not cooperating with her. Her feet, the part of her self. She was part of her existence. She is a girl, the aspirations of which are nature's trust. Those aspirations are not visible. What is visible is only our daughter.

"Her eyes must have been meeting mine; Her eyes were scared. She wanted to say something, something different that doesn't happen in our homes. She was looking for a mother in me, but I had the only wife in me. I was attached to my husband's bed.

I knew that. It was my rite.

My inner mother was never happy with me. What was needed in the mother of a daughter was not visible to me. I was aware of that too.

Standing away from the feeling of victory or defeat, my dilemma, my daughter refused to accept. I was feeling guilty. I knew that every woman's first duty is to be a mother—the mother who is not limited to giving birth only.

I moved slowly close to her bench. I did not talk to her again. Thrusting my hand under her arm, I helped her stand up. Trembling listlessly, she stood up. I said, "Hambrai" (O my), but the girl did not respond. I held her hand and made her walk in step with me. Without wishing and without resisting, she began to walk along. My elder son met us on the way. He did not come towards us, nor did he follow us when we passed by him.

The absence of the sparrow. She did not belong to us, was ultimately proved. In what way was she related to this house? Had she been connected in any way, would she have done this? The taste of my mouth had gone insipid. Who could be trusted these days? The wretched one did not even think that had we not saved her at that time, she would have died or washed away in the rain or burnt by lightning. Even a kite or a falcon could have devoured her. No one knows. Crows and dogs keep swarming around all the time in society.

We had reached in time, to our good fortune. Wherefrom had the enemy of our life, mortal one, come to us, separated from her flock. Our kindness to her has made us suffer now. If the mortal one had not come to our house, it would not have caused us mortal fear. I couldn't do anything for her. She had never demanded anything, perhaps. She might have chirped in her lingua, which I could not have understood. But I can know very well what is in Daman's mind. She does not tweet. If society has turned against her ruthlessly today, she is under her mother's shelter, but why.....? I fail to understand who, among our relatives, is on which side in this conflict between a mother and society.

We were before the shop. Narangi was still busy watching the fish. The cell in my purse was ringing. I left Daman's hand and put the cellphone to my ear.

"We'll take another hour. We have not yet bought it. Let Daman say 'yes' – Why waste money unnecessarily? We will have to throw out the old cage. Yes, yes—I'll use the card. I won't have so much cash in my purse. I don't know how much is the bill for groceries. Don't talk much. …..What does the doctor know? I had told you again and again. It is different for me. And also the sparrow—are fed up with your loud talking. Look here. Even we are at fault. And why not? The cage door was left ajar. Who cares for the trust these days? All right. You need not quarrel now. We will talk later." I put the cell back in my purse.

Perhaps I was about ten years old at that time. Sitting on the string cot, I was doodling on my slate when my uncle raised his hand hurriedly, and a flying sparrow had come into his fist. The sparrow was brought back to consciousness after a great deal of effort. My uncle had got tired of putting drops of water into its half-open beak Grandmother had gone on chiding him again and again. When the crying sparrow regained her consciousness, she flew away with a flutter. The fluttering sound before the flight was so loud. That rustling still echoes in my ears. It was just like a heavily clothed girl, running towards the dark well, had turned into a sparrow and flown away. The sparrow came. After it regained her old liveliness, she passed away; no one knows where—She might have gone beyond the boundaries. Happy she was, and so were we. My uncle, of course, remained upset for some days. But Jani did not fly, nor did we make her fly. The ceiling of our house had become the sky. What had she seen under the roof? She knew everything that took place under this ceiling. She has gone away today, slurring our faces. How would we show our face to those who come to enquire about her? We can't say the tongue-less creature has died. It would have been better if she had died. The dignity of our house would have remained safe. We would have endured her loss.

"Look here, Daman, how lovely are the sparrows this side!" Daman threw a glance at the sparrows – green and red, looking at their buyers. A pale green grape looking sparrow had become quite restive. She was drawing our attention to herself by striking her beak again and again against the cage; she was enticing customers. She was the costliest.

"What's the name of this, Monica," I asked the sale girl, reading her name on the plate.

"Christie," said Monica with a smile. "Christie is the glory of our shop. That's why it is the costliest. Ninety-nine plus tax."

Monica began to praise it for promoting its sale.

She also showed us a matching cage to turn our double-mindedness into a single one. It was for 50 $ plus tax. There was a bar in the cage for Christie to perch on. Special feed, hyper tablets, a little bowl for water, all put together would go to become the decoration piece of the house, but the total cost would have exceeded three hundred dollars. Kulwant did not care for money. All that he wanted was that his daughter should not feel sad. He had decided that the sparrow alone should not be kept; its mate sparrow should also be followed to ward off its loneliness. It was his point that Jani would not have flown away if she had her mate with her.

My elder son had not entered the shop until then.

He had gone after his father. Like a black bee—

"Is it the age for that?—A child does not know how to fasten its belt at this age….."

"Dad, she is my friend, just a friend."

"Talk sense, you idiot. You have just been born and talking about the girl. You don't know the meaning of a friend. Friendship with a girl is a bad thing, you pig."

The elder son had learned no lesson from the slaps, nor had he minded. He did not dial 911 or received the warning. Kulwant slapped him a few times and then got fed up. The elder son thought that he had crossed a hurdle. Kulwant was right. He had his father's right over him. Things had come to such a pass that their relationship had ended.

"Now let me know, my child, Daman, which of the sparrows would you prefer? And what do you think of Christie? It is just like Jani, naughty. See her hopping again and again, here and there, like Jani. Her beak is also like that of Jani's. Colors slightly differ. Jani was pale with a bit of a grape tinge, and she is grape with a yellow shade."

"I don't want a sparrow, mom." She lifted her seemingly swollen feet off the floor and moved behind Christie's cage. I was watching her movements. She moved Christie's cage a little when she got close to it. Christie turned back at once.

"Look, mom," said she in a shrill voice.

"What?" I asked her in surprise. It seemed to me that Daman had talked after a gap of centuries."

"This Christie is not trusting me…That's great—I like it." I failed to understand her philosophy.

"What are you saying?" I said by twisting my brows.

"Look, mom. I shook the cage. The beauty thought that I was going to attack her. Jani was not like her."

She replied to me, thus dilating on Jani's faithlessness also.

"When Christie gets to know you, it would learn to trust you too."

"Mom, you know me. Dad knows me. But no one trusts me except my brother. All of you want to make good the loss that has taken place in the house. It's not what I wish or likes. I do not want to have a sparrow or anything like it. But if still you are bent upon wasting your money, you can buy Christie because she looks straightforward to me. Not like you guys—a double standard. Buy the cage also. I will not give her an empty cage. Who knows, the wretched one might return when in trouble."

Tears began to flow down her cheeks, profusely.

The elder son was still outside. I nodded Narangi towards me and said to her,

"How do you like Christie, Narangi?"

"I don't care. I would say leave this Christie and buy these fish. It would cost less without the risk of its flying back to the sea. How can you trust a sparrow? Leave the door open a bit, and it flies away, fluttering its feathers—It seems we encage it forcibly for the sake of our pleasure, to decorate our house. Where would the low fish go? Going to one side of the fish tank is the one-way path.

….striking against its wall and again to the other side. Drink water and remain content. They die quickly. Change them like changing water. Throw away the dead ones, and bring in new ones of new colors. They won't make us cry like Jani."

How big meaning was there in Narangi's small talk! If I tell someone that Narangi has said all this, no one would believe me.

"Daman, go and call your brother in."

As soon as he came in, my elder son said,

"I don't give a dam. Do as you like."

He had no interest, neither in Christie nor its cage nor in anything concerning the house. He was living in a house like a traveler. Only I knew this. Once, he had shared his mind with me. His days in the house were just numbered. He would fly away in September with the Spanish Dabby. He would be eighteen in September. It was just a small thing when Kulwant talked big. I am also to blame. The entire blame lies on me squarely. When Kulwant returned after a week, he was red with rage because he could not find his over left scotch. He went to the elder son's room. His quilt was not properly folded. Kulwant did not mind minor disorders. He said abruptly,

"You rascal! I am counting the days when you will be eighteen in September. According to law, even midnight is the right time to throw away your belongings, but I grant you twelve hours more. You will remember this gesture, I'm sure."

The elder son got furious. Kulwant had said later on that he had just said those words without meaning anything. But the elder son had felt so deeply in his heart. When he talked to me, he shed more tears than the words he uttered. After all, he, too, was a Jat. Sometimes he used to say, "I'm a native Jat."

But how should we resolve the elder son's tangle? I also did not care much. My worry was limited to my hemicrania and Daman.

I had been slapped several times. Being hit by Kulwant makes me calm as if I take a barefoot walk on grass wet with dew. I feel much obliged to him when Kulwant slaps me. I am being enabled to repay my debt in this way. With the increasing facilities becoming available at home, I feel getting mentally burdened. But the slaps are a boon to me. Sometimes I think restive as if the slapping had become overdue, in the same manner as the hemicrania seems so soothing to me. This ache returns every other day. I take medicine. Migraine runs parallel to my zeal, like the two banks of a river. I get worried when I do not get this ache as if my life is in danger. Some distant one is trying to forget me.

No, I will die without this hemicrania. The germs reared in the head may cluster elsewhere. I keep these germs secured in my head. I have learned how to bear this headache. I had known this when I left my childhood behind. But I took no tablet at that time. It was not the time to take pills. I was capable then of enduring something.

Take a tablet, tie up your head tightly, two hours of rest in the darkroom, and my headache disappeared. Once I was in a deep sleep like this. The germs in my head had not yet been calmed fully when the telephone rang. I turned towards the phone. After two rings, someone had picked up the receiver on the ground floor. Daman was the only one at home. As she moved the cage, a sweet tune was heard. Daman brought this bell with a gift. Whenever Jani and Daman felt happy, they rang the bell and sang to this tune. Jani was given a hyper tablet also. Jani had this tablet as if grabbing out of Daman's hand. It seemed as if this music had some spiritual contact between Jani and Daman. As if Daman and Jani had set a colorful spinning wheel in the village belles spinning party and absorbed in its purring, they were flown to some other world. Or Jani had passed Daman to high skies; such lands were no restrictions, where flights are undertaken according to the seasons. She went to A country that has no name. Which has no borders? Without the barbed wire or the shadow of guns – where there is earth, there is the sky.

And there is the freedom to be happy. This land of mine has been left behind. Left far behind, but its existence never goes away. Sometimes Daman creates this music turning the cage by half As if saying, Let's go there where all the people are our own.

I tried to dose off again by putting the pillow over my head. Still, after the ring from Peter, the music begun by Daman, and Jani's chirping, my sleep got displeased with me. The noise in the living room disturbed me. The elder son was not home on that day. This hooter too had to be heard in our house one day.

Neither he nor I knew what was to follow December. We had not tried to create a feeling of trust in him. As taught in the school, his feelings of self-respect had been shattered again and again in this house. A hundred pitchers full of water were about to be poured on Kulwant's plans, of which only I knew. A mother herself had opened the cage of mind. I could very well imagine his agony. I didn't want my son to also suffer from hemicrania. I would not have been pained at his leaving the house. I don't know why? It appeared to be the right thing, in a way. The only thing I wanted was that wherever he goes, he should keep in touch with me. His flight should not be like that of Jani.

Kulwant's anger hitch was about to come, and the dwindling desire of

life to be destroyed thereby--somewhat decreasing the burden of the soul—
was like the rivers going to be dry. As if the punishment for an imagined
kiss should be a one-sided headache. My hemicrania had begun—the ache
which soothes. The soothing tells me that life is out of danger. It's the only
migraine. Nothing so serious. The desire to live has not yet been destroyed
fully. Thoughts of the elder son were acceptable to me.

Narangi had preferred fish to the sparrow. His choice could be ignored.
After all, he was so young, hardly of nine years. The family needed a
challenge. A sparrow, which could fly, but which we did not let fly, giving
her all the comforts. Her heart may want to fly, but her mind scolded her.

"Are you mad? Where will she go?" I thundered to my tears. These
tears say something in my ears and receive a bad signal. Some cruel people
clip the wings of birds so that they cannot fly. Perhaps they do not know
how to play, or they do not like to play. But our house doesn't have such a
practice. Kulwant being with us, we did not need to clip the wings of any
sparrow. It might be Jani, Christie, or Daman.

We have an army. We have a captain. Why does Kulwant not think
that, besides being a captain, he is a human being also? He is a very decent
person, but he does not know that he is also a human being. He pays no
heed to me. I have told him many a time that he is a very good person.
But he just laughs away.

I have got entangled in other things. All this is about a woman, not
about Kulwant's wife. It was about Daman. She was sad, very sad. Why
had Jani left her? Jani, who had flown out of the open door of the cage in
the closed room and had perched on Daman's shoulder when Daman was
trying to open the lids of her black and blue eyes. That was the day when
a stranger man came out of Kulwant's body and conveying his culture to
a girl who never sees India before. It was a man, not a dad, who beat a girl,
not his daughter. Yes, it was about Daman, who was having jumps. Now
in the sixteenth year and in no time like winking of an eye, she was in the
eighteenth year. Kulwant was afraid of these hops and jumps.

I had bought Christie along with the cage.

Kulwant would have been angry.

He wanted a pair to be believed. He had his thinking. But the manner
of keeping the birdcage in the house, its nicety, a fragrance, all this civility
had no meaning for Kulwant. Sometimes I felt pity for Kulwant. This

feeling turned into love also though I used to get eroded in the process. Narangi held the cage, but Daman raised her seemingly swollen feet and took hold of the pen. Just in the manner as she had held the corpse of the dead sparrow.

Daman watched TV when her friends came to inform her that a grey bird was lying dead on the way. Because of Jani, all of them wanted to convey this to Daman. Daman appeared to all of them, such a sensitive girl. Daman went with her friends and brought back the dead sparrow.

"This sparrow seems to have come from India, an aunt. It seems it got tired of having a very long flight and then died."

They say, "The sparrows of this color are found in India only."

Marlene gave a jolt to me by saying so. Just before the door of the house, Daman dug a small pit. She brought out Jani's cage. Jani could also see the dead body of the gray sparrow. Then Daman and her friends buried the gray sparrow. Daman planted a rose on the spot the next day. That was not the proper place to plant a rose. Kulwant had said nothing. One has to approve of many things which children do.

Daman would take out Jani's cage to that tomb, but Jani's eyes showed no uneasiness, no sadness, no feelings, no sense of belonging to that mud. What Daman was trying to convey to Jani was not getting by her. I was observing all this. Strange earth, strange grass, unusual rose, and grass stalks had no affinity with the tomb.

I felt as if the tomb built in Kulwant's house was not the real one that Jani had not accepted. But this is her father's house. Jani did not like Daman's illogical sentiments for a stranger's dead body and the tomb, nor was it acceptable to her. Daman and Jani, both friends, differed on this issue.

Such rues and differences do happen in childhood. I, too, used to get lost in those rows. Mother would churn the curd. A row of sparrows would come to sit on the parapet. One of the sparrows we called Bhabro was quite merry. She would come to perch on Mother's shoulder now and then. Mother would begin to laugh. When the mother smiled, all faces bloomed. Flying off the mother's shoulder, Bhabro would join her fellow sparrows to pick up grain. Our courtyard blossomed with their presence. This bloom showed on my face too. Behind these sparrows, master Rana would stand with his brass jar, waiting for the buttermilk to be ready. His and my attention used to be fixed in the sparrows. The messages of both of us would get entangled in the sparrows' feathers. The sparrows with such small bellies would be satiated in no time and flutter and fly. Master Rana never tried to move forward even softly as he feared the sparrows would fly away when he moved. The sparrows' coming at the fixed time was the routine, which no one is coming to fetch buttermilk could disturb. No one in the courtyard ever tried to feel concerned as to where Bhabro and her companions had gone in their flight. But it was inevitable that the next day the whole flock would come to sit on the parapet. Bhabro would get perched on the mother's shoulder. Mother would laugh. Bhabro would fly after filling her belly. When we interfere unnecessarily in the working of nature, we lose balance. I, too, could not bear the slight drizzle. They say that a hen used to lay a golden egg. I also felt greedy. The greed became desirous of something more than the golden egg.

"Where does Bhabro live, mom?" I said, looking towards master Rana

"Bhabro has not given me her permanent address. I'll ask her tomorrow." mother had a hearty laugh after saying this. Seeing her happy, I got a little more insistent. I said,

"I'll go after them and find out."

The master hesitated a bit, filling his jar with buttermilk-My golden egg got split and scattered.

"Sit down now, don't be smart. Look at her going after Bhabro, as if were related to her!"

Who had called from the skies? Let him be happy who had called.

Bhabro would come and go away, but what has this heartless Jani done? Thankless Jani. Causing so much pain to my daughter, she has never happened to enquire about her. Daman still goes about carrying the empty cage.

"It has cost two hundred and sixty dollars in all." I was rendering an account to Kulwant.

"Doesn't matter. My Daman should be happy. Are you happy now, my child?" he asked Daman.

Daman put her swollen foot on the plastic table. She gestured that she was better than before.

"She too has begun to talk with gestures like Jani. Did you incite Daman's feet today?"

Telling me about the change he had seen in Daman, he enquired about the fomentation.

"Not yet," I Said, showing my emptiness. I never called Kulwant by name. I always said 'Ji' (A word of respect suffixed to a name but prefixed to a reply." Even when I thought of him contemptuously, this word remained in my mind. Kulwant had said to me many times that while at home, I should address him by name. And in romantic moments, he insisted on this. He would beg softly in my ear to utter his name. But this double standard had never moved my rock-like mind. Instead of love, I uttered the word "Ji" as if taking some revenge. Seriously speaking, I do not love him. I just respect him. Respect–to which he has all the right. After all, he took lavaan (circumambulations around the Holy Book at the time of Sikh marriage) with me. I would avenge my humiliation by saying "Ji" sternly. I said 'Ji' before his family and my own too. I used to cover up the nudity of my spirit in this way. It was a mental victory for me.

Kulwant adored Daman. Perhaps he could not love anyone as much as he did, Daman.

Kulwant's world was tied with Daman. He paid full attention to everything of interest to Daman, howsoever small it may be. Daman asked for a Phulkari (A red scarf embroidered with silk thread for the bride). Kulwant got mad to procure it. The glory of our culture – Phulkari- and who asked for it? – Daman. Phulkari came from India by air. He would put a wad of dollars in Daman's pocket.

Kulwant never talked adequately to his elder son as if he would be expelled from the house. Both father and son would have been free after a year. Things taking a drift came to such a pass one day when the elder son thwarted his attempt to slap me when he had raised his hand. Pushing aside the slapping hand, he threatened to call the police also. This was not proper for him. He had exceeded his limit. His love and affection for his mother had clashed with Kulwant's wife. No one liked the conflict in the house. Even Jani had raised her voice against this with her chirps. Now I am thinking with whom had Jani sided while chirping, Kulwant, or the elder son? She was an eyewitness to anything happening in our living room.

To my mind, the elder son thwarting the attempt to slap me was an intrusion on my rights. A great disrespect is shown to Kulwant's wife. The elder son appeared to be a stranger, totally unconversant with the house's mannerism and customary practices. Even Daman had felt bad. Narngi was lost in watching the Simpson show. Daman drew a long breath. Never before had she breathed like this. She felt a great burning in her seemingly swollen feet. She sat down on the sofa with a knife in her hand. Kulwant was not at fault; it was certainly an excess on the part of the elder son. I felt as if Babaji's picture on the wall also had got twisted. What kind of twist is this?

Kulwant had returned home after five days from his business trip. He was unable to find a quarter of the bottle lying in the house. The liquor store was closed on Sunday. I had not been able to take care of that quart. Amid showers of abuse, I thought that he should finish with the slap as soon as possible. After this, Kulwant used to get calm. And so did I. But the elder son had upset the equilibrium. In the lull before the storm, only Jani's chirping was echoing. But the mortal Jani proved to be worse than humans. Daman could bear anything but not separation either of dad or Jani.

"Mom, when would Dad return from India?" Daman had asked with so much eagerness when her feet were still standard.

"I want him to bring a drum for me from India."

"For what?"

"I have promised it to Peter for his birthday."

Daman had taken some liberty after Kulwant had gone. I thought there was no harm. After all, Peter was his classmate, and he was a Punjabi too. So what if he was not a Jat? They were just friends and not lovers. If I stop them, they will meet stealthily. If they steal, they might break the friendship. I did not question her even about wearing clothes of her choice. What is the use if a child changes dress when at school? But Kulwant had no clue of this. We, mother and daughter, would not have told him. But this mention of a drum divulged the secret. Just a beat echoed so high. Kulwant was furious with rage, and Daman drew inward her small head, which she had raised a little bit. Kulwant slapped the cage with both hands. Jani's chirping rose sky-high. I knew that the wailing and crying girls do not harm. After all, Daman was my flesh and blood. Kulwant stopped going out of town and also stopped Daman's going out of the house.

Daman and Jani's friendship grew more profound. Jani and Daman had been friends for five years. Daman was at the last phase of childhood when Janni came into our life.

We lived in the apartment in those days. One day we were having a stroll in the rear of the building when we met Jani standing on the footpath. It was a one and a half feet pathway made in the grass by those going for a walk. It was meant only for human beings. The birds flew over or sat on the grass. The humans threw away the crumbs of bread in the grass. It was like a compromise. The footpath is ours, and the grass for you. But Jani sat on the way and not grass. Breaking of the center like this by a bird looked so odd. It was not a regular thing. We got on our toes. Tip-toeing, we were very slow in the hope that she would understand our humanism. She would fly back to the world of her birds. But this did not happen. She did not fly. Nor did she move away. It seemed she had lost hope for life. The indecision about life and death had tied her feet.

The yellow feathered Jani was nice to look at, but otherwise, she seemed to be sad. We drew quite close to Jani and sat down, surrounding her. When Kulwant extended his hand, she fell on his palm listlessly. Daman rushed to the tap in the park and brought water for her in her cupped hand. Jani, straightening up in Kulwant's palm, began to drink water with her tiny beak. When she had drunk water, Daman opened her cupped-hand. Jani got into Daman's little palm. I was surprised. Kulwant's palm was broad and strong. Leaving aside the safer place, why did Jani prefer the little palm? Daman's eyes were full of surprise and immense happiness too. Letting it sit in Daman's palm, we brought home the yellow sparrow.

We did not know where the sparrow come from, which was unable to walk, had begun. Did it come from which land? Do they churn curds in the large earthen vessels in that land? Did anyone come with a jar for buttermilk in the morning there? Did anyone keep awake the whole night waiting for buttermilk? I did not know all this. Still, I was looking at the yellow sparrow. I thought if the sparrow had a parapet under her, she would not have come to Canada.

But the question that arose was why did it get separated from the flock. And why had she called so upset after separating? Even her wings appear to be disheveled. Some ungrateful people had dealt with this sparrow very severely. I knew that. Why don't these self-willed sparrows see reason when still there is time. If they take proper care of themselves, no one can change their name. Because of ignorance alone, any Tom Dick or Harry can give them any name. They don't have their last name, for sure. Any useless person can hold them by their nose ring and write his name after theirs. And they tolerate this quietly. We, too, gave the name of "Jani" to the yellow sparrow.

Jani's old history ended with this christening. A superior cage, matching Jani's feathers, was bought. Kulwant had once brought something like this for me. It might be suitable for physical pleasure, but I wouldn't say I liked all this. But I am deeply in love with Kulwant's aspirations.

Kulwant and Daman had gone there to buy all this. Kulwant had taken off that day, especially for the sake of his daughter. Just in the center of the cage was kept a wicker-bed for Jani to sit on.

"Have you seen the result of separating from the flock?" Why did Kulwant repeat this within my hearing day and night, I did not know. Daman got lost in Jani's chirping. And I, in his taunts. It seemed as if Daman had tilted all her love for Peter into Jani's being. What kind of mental makeup was it which had sprung in Daman after me? At Kulwant's decision to commit suicide because of Peter, Daman felt as if her feet had swollen. She strolled. Slower than me even. Just like encaged Jani. I took her to the doctor. She had no ailment. It was only fear psychosis. Yes, the fear of swelling of feet. Fear of inability to walk. As if her feet would split if she walked fast. Jani had been in this house for five years.

Bhabro, the sparrow, stood in my memory, with her head raised. The coming of sparrow Bhabro, and going of sparrow Bhabro were my sinful moments. Those moments had again come alive. I opened Jani's cage, placed Jani slowly on my palm, and made it sit as usual on the fireplace, and I began to clean the cage. Jani flew and sat down on the TV. Flying from the TV, she came to sit on my shoulder. Daman was still asleep. Perhaps Jani got a golden chance by looking into Daman's eyes. She would not have become so audacious. The outer door was open. We had a fixed alarm system in the house. It was meant for unwelcome trespassers from outside. It was never thought that there should be an alarm system for those stepping out of the threshold of this house. If such an eventuality had been thought of, Kulwant certainly would have imported the instrument from America. He went to America almost every week. Science has made great strides. That alarm would have caught Jani at once. I would have twisted her wings forcibly. Or I might not have done this. Perhaps the alarm would not have been heard. What would this non-hearing have given me? Peace, or tension, I do not know? Certain things are never understood.

Flying away from my shoulder, she went out and sat upon the little tomb under the rose. I felt horrified. It was a real horror. It is supposed sometimes. It seems to be my own, this horror!

Master Rana had never married. There was nothing like that--but he is still alive. I realized my mistake momentarily. Soon I controlled myself. It can't be.

Jani will come back to the cage. That I had been shut in this cage for forty-two years, I had never thought. Daman grew up playing with her toys or other games and got imprisoned in the same cage. She had never thought of this. Nor had I ever thought that, after all, I was a mother. I have some duty. I can realize Daman's anguish. Why don't I do then? And where could Jani have gone? We had brought her when she was almost dead. We loved her so much. Where would she go now? Are the shackles of love and respect meant for human beings only? My mind began to tell me that she would not come back to the cage. I imagine now that Jani was before my eyes at that time, and why then had I begun to think that she would not come back? Was it already there in my subconscious mind that Jani should actually fly away in the free air?

The cage is a cage, after all.

Had this notion come to stay in a nook of mind that Daman may go to Peter. We will face it. Time will solve all this. I became terrified.

Kulwant would say, you failed to take care of a sparrow. How would you look after your daughter? I rushed to Daman's bedroom. She was not asleep. She was frowning at the ceiling, her eyes wide open. Seeing me in a worried state, she stood up. I told her everything. She began to laugh.

She said, "Mom, don't worry. Jani will not go anywhere."

Daman put on her slippers. She stepped out with me. Jani was not there near the tomb. We went out and looked around. Jani had perched on the roof.

Daman cast an angry glance at Jani, and opening her palm, she said, "Jani, come here."

Jani always obeyed Daman when she was in the cage. Daman had once insisted also on freeing Jani to fly in the open air. We had brought a bird feeder from the Wall-Mart. These feeders of different designs were not very expensive. Squirrel Scanner was worth six dollars only.

"Come, bhaji (brother) bite your snack." Pointing to a squirrel.

When Kulwant said this, all those in the house, including an elder son, had a hearty laugh. But today, Jani enjoying the open air, did not look at the bird feeder even once. When we had brought the bird feeder, we had not trusted Jani. Even after five years' association, we were afraid that she might not come back if we let her go out in the open. This bird feeder was for untamed birds. I wanted her to sit on the bird feeder just for once, pick up her grain, fill her belly, and then decide. Wrong decisions are taken on an empty stomach. But Jani was in a hurry. There was something more important than eating.

Jani ignored what Daman had said. Daman ran inside and brought out the full container of hyper tablets. Jani saw the tablet on Daman's palm. Jani took a small flight and again got perched on the roof. Daman's wrath was on the increase. She looked like Kulwant when she was angry, and Kulwant looks like his father in anger. Jani flew, took a round of Daman's head, and then she flew higher and higher and got lost in the clouds, out of sight.

The new sparrow was not feeling at home in the new place. Christie was quite frolicsome at the shop, but the new house and the original cage were not her likings. Daman also did not care. Perhaps an ill wind was blowing in the place. There was a new trouble every other day. Sometimes it was between the elder son and father, and sometimes it was Peter's phone call, which caused turmoil in the house.

I was not in a position to make any decision. What authority did I have except a new idea given to me by Jani? She was not a traveler. Why did she go away then? In what condition was she five years ago when she had come to us? Perhaps she was a mother whose daughter's feelings were being trampled underfoot, or she was a daughter who had rebelled against her father and then could not bear the burden thereof on her mind. And then she got quite thick with Daman. But the heart's river is deeper than seas, and who knows what afflicts the heart? When she got the chance, the old world pulled her to its side. Have I forgotten my childhood? Not at all.

What have I gained by being sacramental? What sort of world I have, where my daughter is unhappy, my son is unhappy, I am unhappy, and

Kulwant also is unhappy? Who is inflicting unhappiness on all of us and snatching from us our fresh air? Then I concluded. Perhaps Jani had gone to enquire about her daughter. Though her life was in danger, she endangered it further. What standing is there for the sparrows separated from the flock? She would not survive. But still—

"Daman, your dad says that Peter does not belong to our community. Does he belong to a low caste? Who are they, Peter and his people?"

After having our dinner and sitting on the sofa, opposite Kulwant, and within his hearing, I had said this with all the boldness. The elder son was not there. I wanted his absence. I did not want him to help me in any way, nor was I in a mood to accept anyone's help.

"What is this caste?" Daman's innocent question was not permeating the pores of my body.

"Shall I tell you what caste is?" said Kulwant looking at both of us threateningly.

The next day when Kulwant was not in, I locked the house, considering it as a cage. Kulwant was compelled to ponder for the first time. Either us…or your traditional belief— Such rotten ideas which have lost their significance. Leaving the corpse of the dead understanding….. in that dying house, I flew away, as Jani had done.

Walking in step with my daughter's find, to make her head high, I was feeling a lot better in the fresh air.

Kulwant's melting point would be so low, and I had never imagined. He was sacrificing everything; all the money, the entire house, was being offered to us, put in an earthen pot, wrapped in a red cloth, the small bowl.

Whose ashes are these?

It was just an obduracy. A hardened stance – I won't accept this."

He may not commit suicide. I feared sometimes. Kulwant had said so many times. Let him do if he so desires. I don't care. Who is responsible for the suicide which I had committed, years ago, centuries ago? O ye Kulwant, the pyre of your thinking needs to be burnt. Another Sita would be born out of this fire. How long would Ahalya live like a stone?

He might see reason. He might not.

Jani has also gone out looking for something 'Just possible.' Now I wonder why Jani had preferred Daman's palm to Kulwant's broad and robust hand when she had met us for the first time.

FORBIDDEN FRUIT

S HERA ANGRILY OPENED the door. "Aren't you going to the party?" Bibi asked, "I don't think your symptoms are telling."

Shera hit the work bag on the sofa.

"Son, if you listen to me, don't go. Whenever you are in a bad mood, there is always a problem.

Shera looked at her mother and then lowered his eyes.

Taking the towels, he saw Sandeep lying face down on the bed.

She didn't notice Shera's presence, which made Shera even angrier. He took his underwear out of the cover, dropped it on his shoulder, and went to the washroom.

He was hyper while brushing. Bibi also knew that there would be an attack, and Sandeep was also waiting.

The two were in deep thoughts, and Shera came out after taking a bath.

Contrary to Sandeep's thinking, Shera said, "Get ready now. Are you waiting for Christmas?"

"My mood is not well; you can't go alone?"

Saying "no," Shera went down the stairs.

Bibi was lying on her head down. She looked at Shera and said, "like the tea, son?"

"No, Bibi, I took coffee on my way home."

Meanwhile, Sandeep came down and opened the cover and took out Advil's bottle.

There was tension on Bibi's face; she said in unison, "Look, Shera, if Sandeep is loose, then you should go alone and come soon. Tell everybody that Bibi is sick."

"Oh God, I am sick and tired now from life," Shera said.

"Sandeep took the pill and go to her room. The clock was ticking."

Shera got ready and went into the room and said, "Do you remember the night when I needed you, and your behavior was so scary?"

"Yes, I have not forgotten anything. Why don't you understand? Days are not always the same."

"I want to hold you in the same arms even today, the whole universe ... kindness... I want love from you that will never end but no matter if it is not like that, then deny that which is not right. We have certainly changed."

"Without your love, I have become stronger. It's as if Budha's philosophy is coming into me."

Sandeep was speaking in profound silence. Silence is so loud Shera could realizing this.

Picking up the keys, Shera said, "Thank you, you have taken my thoughts to the sky even beyond the sky. Thank you, Sandeep."

Sandeep looked at Shera and smiled. Seeing her smile, Shera said, "It is good to look across the sky without knowing, but I am afraid that the gravity of your body will not attract me again."

Shera was looking at her as if she didn't understand anything. He felt as if the side of the scales he was sitting on had risen too high. It would have been better if I had lived in a thicker place.

He spoke like a loser and a weary bird, "Love is meaningless if your pride and decency do not remain."

"I want to live on earth and enjoy my family traditions; what is wrong with it?" Sandeep said.

"This is your thinking, but the experience will one day teach you which is the right path. The right path is always difficult, but the Comfort Zone does not allow us to choose that path."

Shera left, and Sandeep got involved in deep thoughts. She remembered how Shera used to treat her.

Reluctantly, she pulled out her Diary. In which her islands were buried. She never dared to share the Diary with Shera.

She did not write daily but only when something different happened.

Twenty years ago, he heard the echo of her uncle in his Diary.

"What she did? Anybody could make this kind of mistake. Parents have to cover-up. She is our daughter. I will make her understand. She respects the traditions."

"You keep quiet and stay away from this matter. "Shut up, great donor!"

You are a mother, all your fault. Your duty to keep an eye on what society would say now. family's names would be ruined forever."

"Send her out, in any country. She will not survive here. With whom will we be stuck every day?" Uncle pour gasoline of fire.

My whole body was shaking. I agreed with the family for abortion. My body was fragile for the last two weeks, and now this is family talk that makes me sick and tired.

It was summertime and sweltering days when I got married." The stranger's name was Jagsher Singh.

The family is pleased; relatives are jumping with joy. Even in the lust of marriage, I was in a sad mood. The next one came from Canada; how could he be so stupid?

"Sat Sri Akal Ji," Shera spoke for the first time.

It seemed to me that it would soon lose its appeal. My heart was pounding.

"So cute! So beautiful! Amazing, he was praising my beauty. I was scared to listen to these words. I kept quiet, and then he said, "Why are here only have six weeks? I am damn lucky to get such a beautiful girl, but what beautiful rose did need to decide so soon?"

She could have laughed at the joke, but her fear was not in the mood for a romantic talk. There was a knock on the front door. Shera went and opened the door. Her aunt was smiling outside with boiling milk and said, "Look, Sherya, don't bother our girl too much; look how innocent like goat she is."

"No, Bhuva Ji, you know my nature."

Aunt returned on her feet.

She made up her mind to say the first thing and said, "Yes, your aunt is wonderful, and their daughter looks very heavenly."

"Yes, Sandeep Sweety also belongs to your community in color."

Hearing the sweet compliment, I fell silent.

Jagsher said, "When I found out that you have mastered in your philosophy, I had decided that even if the girl is deaf, I have to do it, but your eyes are gorgeous!"

This is my favorite topic. It will be very nice when two people get together with the same belief."

I was encouraged to hear that. Maybe my eyes will cover me, what more do I need?

"I think you are very interested in philosophy."

"Yes, Sandeep, philosophy is my favorite subject."

"Yes, I have not only mastered but also done M. Phil. My dissertation was related to child psychology."

"It is simply more exciting for me. I wish I could master this subject too."

"Then why did you go to Canada?" People go there only for a lot of money and comfort."

"No doubt, but I had other reasons."

"Thank God for connecting with an interesting person." My mind was at the moment when he was about to take off my clothes.

I had to clear my throat. My jewelry had to be sorted one by one. I was supposed to take off the Phulkari lime on my head, but he didn't do anything with his hands and said, "Sandeep, it's very hot. You take off this heavy cloth and go easy. Then we talk a lot."

"I wiped the sweat on my forehead with a towel and got out of bed. I took two pieces of transparent nightie out of my red briefcase and went to the washroom.

"Subhan Allah! he praised my physical beauty in terms of how much he was feeling. Now it was only a matter of time before my allegory began.

The flowing waters had to pass under the bridges once again.

The artist inside me was ready for that. I came and sat on the bed stage and sat down with the headboard covered.

"Sorry for the inconvenience. Shera joked and got up and went to the washroom. I waited as hard as a mountain for him to come back. I wanted what was to happen as soon as possible.

Shera also got dressed in pajamas and came and said, "Princess is very hot outside, but Manali is on the inside.

"Yes, that's all my union turned out to be a beautiful couple." I thought that Shera is also proud of himself; that's why he has said he is proud.

"Sandeep! "I was daring to look at him," he said patiently.

"You must have read about the 'unlearn concept of Buddhism', what would you like to say about it?"

"All I know is that nothing is practical; everything is bookish," I said sweetly.

"No, Sandeep, I don't think so. These bibliographies are practical, and I am committed to them."

I lowered my eyes. I don't know where my fake smile came. I just smiled but said nothing.

"Are you my wife now?"

I laughed loudly and said, 'Any doubt!'

"No, No doubt, but only what has been learned after marriage.

I don't think so.

It's one thing to be married and quite another to know each other."

I didn't understand what he wanted, even though my art was not ready for it. I just needed to pass my womanish at that time. I said, "Please call me wife, not friend tonight."

"No, you are not my wife but the woman sitting inside me."

"The concept of a wife is the gift of our subconscious; that's what I'm talking about unleashing; in other words, unlearn yourself, what is inside you by birth by traditions."

"What's the difference? It's just a matter of words."

My mother and many other friends and relatives sitting inside me were amazed.

At last, my mother sitting inside me thought softly, which only I could hear when you don't know what to say, then keep your mouth shut. My artist gave me the same advice.

A sound echoes as it hits a small hill.

"Sandeep, I am a stranger, I don't want to be a stranger to you and you should not be a stranger to me."

My artist accepted the challenge and said, "Yes, that's right, but when do men think that way?"

He answered, "When does a woman think that way?"

Hearing this, I became silent.

"It's not about men and women; it's about a person, a gender. We have a lot to unlearn."

"As you see fit. It looks like I'm fortunate."

"Saying good luck is also a shadow of the rituals you have learned. Let's get rid of our shadows first."

"Yes"

"Sandeep, let's talk about forbidden fruit. Why was this fruit forbidden, and what did God say that Adam and Eve did not accept?"

Things went the other way. My fear also subsided, and I said, "Please start talking. I will listen and answer according to my understanding."

"Yes, lady, why are you walking around naked today?" God spoke.

"It simply came to our notice then. Adam looked at Eve and answered.

"No, you weren't naked before. That is why you are leaning to cover yourself with leaves today." "Indeed, Adam and Eve felt naked and wanted to cover their bodies. It wasn't like that before."

I was speechless and said, "What does that mean?"

"Yes, this is a very big question for you. There is a lot of detail and the answer is even wider. Let's talk about this today."

"Tathastu," I said jokingly.

"This is where our learning process begins, Sandeep."

"How is that?

"The gender of a person comes out through this process. Otherwise, my wife lives in me.

Woman in every part of my body, just like your man is in every aspect of your body.

We have to meet that gender only, not Sandeep to Shera and Shera to Sandeep; we have to find our second half through meditation. Most people called it sex, but this is not sex, the realization of your own. To complete one's journey, this is the only way, not an alternative."

"Oh! Great, I never thought like this before."

"Yes, Sandeep, pleasure is not happiness. Happiness stays forever, but pleasure is momentary."

"Sweet reunion doesn't happen to anyone else, but it does happen only with yourself.

When I meet sweetly, that will be when I meet my inner woman. The sweet meeting will be when you meet the man inside you.

We don't need leaves to meet ourselves."

Shera grabbed and kissed my hand and said, "Right now, this hand is mine, not the air around you. The wind that blows across me is yet to come.

"Sandeep, my daughter, the lunch is ready. Come down. Get it yourself and give it to me too; I'm hungry. "Bibi's voice broke Sandeep's attention, and she closed the Diary.

A dry petal from the hastily closed Diary fluttered and fell on the bed.

"Yes, Bibi, what vegetable should I get?" Potatoes or turnips?"

"Sandeep, there are only a few potatoes, just for one. You give me turnips."

"Yes, Bibi, as you wish."

Sandeep put the chapati and cooked turnips on a plate and handed it to Bibi on the couch.

"If we sleep together when we don't know each other, what's the difference between you and the hooker?"

We will sleep together one day when we will both be full of longing to meet our gender." After eating lunch, Sandeep came up again and opened the Diary.

"It's a lottery for you, Sandeep," I said to myself in my Diary. I was not listening to Shera from heart. I just pretend that I am listening. Going to Canada is my project for totally different thoughts.

I am wondering what would happen if that happened. See you once you get to Canada. I was talking in the mirror, looking at myself. Now the mirror is sitting on my pillow, and my pen is running.

'See dear Diary...

Beware of the whole life came into the hands of someone other than me. I am stupid sometimes; look I am talking to you—same as Shera living in illusions.

This idiot person wants to make me his wife. O fool, with the marriage ceremony, I do not become your wife, how else will I become?

Why do I think you are laughing too, dear Diary? Looks like Al that sounds crap to me,

'I doubt it. Maybe Shera is impotent? Men are nailed with the scent of a woman. Can't her first date start with a sweet meeting? There must be a knob.

He doesn't even look at my limbs!

After two hours of non-sense, he closed the burning lid.

I was scared but still laughed.

I began to wonder what kind of thread my broken spinning wheel was holding, was it a good thing or was it some kind of God's deed that I did not understand. My heart was filled with the fact that I am no longer in love with anyone but full of hatred.

Then why are the dry petals in my Diary? The question within me.

On the wedding night, after Shera slept, I Look at Shera's innocent face with my eyes closed; I fell in love. I thought he was a good man. My thoughts split into two parts.

Maybe his philosophy turns me on.

Let's see, let's hear his philosophy.

Should I take off my necklace before going to bed now?

The day before the wedding, the mother had said, 'Sandeep, trust God. Only with faith in God, you will be blessed. Mistakes are always be ignored if you accept with a true heart.

Why Do You Ask God in Trouble? Why do you ask questions? He knows everything. The world is HIS stage; we are only dolls.

How can HE think that you are unhappy?

Don't be discouraged when a plan or dream doesn't work out. I don't know if anyone said it or I made it up.

I closed my eyes in anticipation of the morning.

On January 4, 2004, Sandeep landed at Calgary YYC International Airport. After clearing from immigration, she walked outside, and Shera waved from a distance. Sandeep breathed a sigh of relief. Her first step was completed.

"Welcome, Sandeep, to our city."

Along the way, he did the traditional things. I asked how everyone was doing and asked about the trip. They reached home. After drinking tea, Shera asked her to take a bath. Sandeep's tiredness was relieved by the shower.

Maybe tonight is my honeymoon, but you know what? This person needs to understand. Sandeep thought.

"The daughter will be tired and hungry. Eat breakfast and rest for a while. Even Shera will not go to work this evening shift."

She remained silent and saw Shera decorated the dining table with the help of Bibi. What a wonderful way to welcome a new member.

Shera grabbed a chair for Sandeep, and Sandeep looked at Shera and smiled. She looked at Shera with tears in her eyes. She realized that Shera is a very good person.

"Bibi Ji, you come too?" Sandeep said.

"No, Sandeep, you eat. I have already eaten." I feel the warmth of a mother."

"Yes, Sandeep, Bibi has eaten, and one more thing, Bibi is a very good cook. All acquaintances praise her."

"Great, Bibi, teach me too. I can cook and cook well, but I will learn from you now."

"Yes, why not? I have ancient recipes taught by my mother-in-law and by her grandmother."

"Sandeep, my grandmother, was literate in her time."

My grandmother did a B.A. in the 1940s in India. Grandma had become the darling of our village. Men also came to consult her. She was very fond of the kitchen, and she made a notebook in which old recipes are recorded. She gave it to my mother, and Bibi may provide you the same notebook, but it depends on how your mother-in-law is doing."

Now it's not just you; she is my mother too."

Shera laughed and said, "When do I say no? Take possession of the mother. If need be, I will get your recommendation."

Bibi stood in the kitchen, laughing and said, "Take my first gift." She put two plates of sugar and sevian on the table.

Sandeep put the first spoon in her mouth and realized that it contained not only sugar but much more. She looked at Bibi with a tasteful mouth and said, "Bibi, you have done a wonderful job."

"Thank you, Sandeep."

"Bibi has one thing to say if you agree."

"Say Sandip; I won't listen to you, then who else will I believe?'"

"Jagsher Ji, you also listen. Bibi is not on my regular accent; it looks like I am pretending to be Bibi. I'm tired of calling you Bibi; it looks like I am pretending. I call my mother, Biji, not Bibi. Can't I call you biji? Is it like talking to my mom?"

"My daughter, what's the point of asking this? You call can me biji."

"Oh, biji !" Sandeep got up, hugged Bibi. Shera's laughter subsided, and he laughed for a long time and said, "Bibi has become two in one from today."

"Good Sandeep, now you go to your bedroom and relax, so much travel you did.

Shera, take Sandeep into the room and put her suitcases in her place, now that is her room. Shera, that was not your room anymore. All you have to do now is ask Sandeep."

"Yes, Bibi, now the owner has come. Let the master take you to your room."

Sandeep got up Sandeep reached for the briefcase, "Oh, Sandeep, stay, I'll bring it." Sandeep laughed and slowly climbed the stairs.

"What will happen, by morning? Sandeep's mind wandered, thinking.

Sandeep climbed one of the steps of the stairs. Sandeep was feeling devastated.

She does not want to be challenged or tested. She also enjoyed all the blessings to be bestowed on her. As she thinks, everything will be completed.

She would never have come to Canada without the thunder.

"Jagsher Ji, I could not have imagined that I would get such a family, very wrong rumors about Canada.

Come on, Sandeep, where did I even think I would get another girl like you?" How could Bibi have felt that she would have a daughter like you?"

Shera started running her fingers through Sandeep's hair.

"Jagsher Ji, I will only call you Shera in solitude. I love being called Shera."

"Yes, I am Shera; we have to become each other."

There were tears in Sandeep's eyes; she thought she would not pretend to be tempted on her own. There is no room for hypocrisy.

"Sandeep, now you try to sleep, after so much fatigue when you take a shower and eat, you fall asleep. We'll talk in the morning now." Shera opened the blanket and gave it to Sandeep and said, let me help Bibi in the kitchen."

Shera left. Seeing her leaving, Sandeep began to think that if you forgive me, I will be your servant for the rest of my life. Sandeep's tears were like pearls, wiped half-digested, and then I don't know when Gudi went to sleep.

Sandeep's tears came into her eyes while she is reading Diary and visualizing the past.

"Hot tea," Sandeep opened her eyes when she heard the voice and looked at Shera, who was standing beside her pillow.

"You slept a full twelve hours. I just got a call for you; I thought the Princess should be picked up."

"Whose phone was it?"

"Of Kuldeep Singh."

"What was that Kuldeep Sir Ji saying?"

"I didn't ask; you just call and ask."

Sandeep was still drinking tea when Shera brought a landline phone and handed it to her and said, let me take a shower; you call, then we will have breakfast. Bibi has made potato pancakes for you today." Shera took a towel and went outside to another washroom.

Sandeep called and went downstairs.

Sandeep was a little upset.

She did not want to see Kuldeep on the first day.

She was also hesitant to ask.

Shera realized that Sandeep wanted to say something and said: "You have talked to Kuldeep, Sir?"

"Yes, that's right, they say, come and meet."

"And what is the problem? I will drop you."

"They invite you too."

"It's hard for me. I'll go with you another day." I need to go to work today."

"No, Shera, I will go with you. They live alone, and I don't want to go alone."

"Isn't Kuldeep a good man?"

"It's not about Kuldeep, Sir, but what do you think?"

"Well, as you say, think, and try. Have breakfast and then we'll talk."

"Sit back, Sandeep."

"Sandeep, you are not my slave; you are my wife," said Shera.

"Yes"

"In India, We also talked about on this topic. We are a gender beyond husband and wife.

Gender within each other. The most important thing to meet your inner self is trust in each other. I believe in this belief as much as I think of my God. It is not right to look to me for everything you do. With traditional slavery, we can never reach the extreme where our inner being can be found. Whenever I have something to say, I will let you know without hesitation.

Kuldeep Sir is your Sir from where you have got academic knowledge. What will they think of their experience? I'm sure you understand. Now you get ready. I will leave you." With that, Shera stepped forward and kissed Sandeep on the forehead.

That night Sandeep was lying in her bed and thinking intensely.

When he saw a man entering the room, Sandeep got out of bed and stood up.

She quickly hugged the man. He put a shower of kisses on Shera's face. A few moments later, Shera turned to close the door, then Sandeep grabbed him again as if to say there is no need to close the door now.

Shera also went back to bed instead of the door.

No frills, no excuses, no hospitality.

Sandeep was getting inside without introducing herself.

Sandeep slept as if he had been sleeping for a long time.

Early in the morning, Sandeep saw that Shera was still asleep.

He wanted to save the moment he had spent.

She took out her Diary and wrote, "I celebrated my honeymoon on June 26 for the first time.

Indeed it was a celebration on earth. I fell in love with Shera before I went to bed."

From now on, this Diary is not mine but his too. Let him know the truth of the Diary.

"No, Sandeep, I can't do that. Diary belongs to you only, your confidentiality.

She closed the Diary and saw at the watch and went downstairs.

"Biji, I'm going to drop Jagga off at school."

"Yes, Sandeep, leave; this is also the fear of tomorrow."

Sandeep put her finger on Jagga, and both the mother and son left for school. Jagga is now five years old. How much water has passed under the bridges within five years? They have now reached another world. Shera's daily liquor filled the whole house with acid.

Sandeep was wondering what was wrong with him? Is it wrong to think of your atomic family?

Sandeep remembered the first night. Then the second and then the third, Shera kept clinging to her. Nights passed, and the years passed. Shera seems to be a resident of another world., then I don't know which sin I have committed. Did I have no obligation to the family? There is so much more to unleash. How can one release a household?

Biji's call came from India, "Yes, Sandeep, what have you done?

"No, I did not talk yet.

You're coming. Talk to Shera diplomatically; I scare to ask."

"You just start the topic, see what they say about this…rest leave on me."

"Oh, mom, not easy for me to talk to Shera. It looks like not right."

"We have to talk; your talk is more impressive; after all, you are his wife. You are so beautiful, Shera dare not to say no to you. Use tricks of the trade; you know what I mean."

"Okay, mom, I would try tonight."

"You should know how and when you talk for complete success. These men are all the same. You know what I mean…"

"Oh, you naughty, look like you always give a hard time to Dad; I will try."

"Okay, I'll talk to you after my job."

"My blessings,"

Sandeep laughed. After hanging up the phone, Sandeep thought that he would talk to Shera today. Shera will not put me down."

The mother and son reached the school and Sandeep's line of thinking was broken.

On the way back, she went to the park on the way. People were walking, and two were jogging. She and Shera used to go jogging in the morning, but now the pairing of flying together is broken.

Sandeep thought about Bibi first, how she used to say that she is a mother and how she started thinking only as Shera's mother. People are telling the truth. Mothers-in-law can never be mothers.

After talking to her mother, she thought that this is a trivial matter. My brother is younger than I am. He goes to the gym; he is just like a model.

He remembered that night. Sandeep, close your eyes; it's a surprise for you. Sandeep noticed that Shera had a transparent nightie in her hand of light brown color.

"I didn't bring this for you."

'Then, for whom?"

"For myself…"

"Sandeep went to the washroom and put on the nightie and walked in front of the mirror.

She came out and said, "A Tan…tran. Tran…tran…" she walked around on her feet.

"My God, maybe I donate pearls lots of pearls." Shera had just said that Sandeep fell on her and her arms gripped Shera. Shera smelled the scent that Sandeep had never used before. Body butter was mixed on the body, which was never applied before.

Shera felt different, but he was on his ride and concentrated only on one object.

"I want to talk to you."

"Later." That's all Shera could say with a fast heartbeat.

"No, sweetheart, right now. Your woman is asking a bit."

"I said, 'no later.'" Shera felt hot and surrendered to the air in the room and fell silent.

"Now tell me what you have to say, what an important task which is disturbing my meditation.

"It's not a joke; it's serious."

"Yes, I have been listening."

"We meet God together. One should also do good deeds for society."

"Yes, of course."

"Why don't we become mediators?"

"Do you mean to associate with God? No problem. It may be God's work, and he wants us to do it."

"Yes, you are right. The fact is that you know that my parents have been medically cleared and will get a visa within two months, but the problem is my brother. He is now thirty years old and is not coming along. Why not find a girl for him?"

"Yes, why not?" He is very handsome. Very quickly, we could find a girl. We ask people around because we should put an add-in matrimonial column in local papers. I wonder how he is still single?"

"Many girls are hanging around, but he wants a Canadian girl, and we have a beautiful girl in our own family."

"Who?"

"Your cousin, sweetie."

"But she is my cousin's sister."

"Yes, she is your cousin. I saw her at my wedding. Sohan, my brother, likes her, and so do my parents."

"Isn't your brain damaged, Sandeep?"

"What's wrong with my brain? My brain is all right.

Can't they get married somewhere, and then why can't they get married to each other?"

"He is your brother, and Sweetie is my sister. Not possible in our traditions. Don't you know that?

"But, you always talk about being unlearned?"

"My unlearned concept does not say that we should not accept the norm of society how we face our society. Do you know what people talk about this? Not possible. Even ask your parents. They don't even accept it."

I don't care what people said?" Sandeep growled.

Shera was upset."So that is why you are different in bed?"

"What do you mean?"

"Nothing"

Shera picked up the keys and walked out. He thought that maybe he could explain his point, but it didn't. Sandeep grabbed the same writ.

By Friday evening, the weekend had begun. The weekend that Shera would have loved like a wedding. In the middle of nowhere, he thought he might meet the woman inside again today, but there was a question lying on the bed.

"When Sandeep saw that Shera was getting romantic, she started talking again.

"Please, this is our bed. We are here two alone—just man and woman, who care for each other. Please don't bring anything on this bed. Don't pollute our bed, Sandeep."

"Humm," Sandeep murmured.

"If you want to talk something else, Let's go to another room."

Shera remembered the red light area. If the room is mine, I'll get two hundred dollars.

It was the same now.

Shera asked, "Will you answer one thing?"

"Ask!" Sandeep murmured.

"If you liked Sweetie so much, why didn't you talk at that time?" Sohan and Sweetie were both unmarried."

"It simply came to our notice now. But what's the big deal?"

"This is not that simple. I can tell you why you are thinking about now."

"Okay, sweetheart, tell me," Sandeep said.

"Sweetie's student visa has turned to PR now. Isn't that true?"

Before Sandeep could answer, Shera himself said, "My God, what did I say? My thinking is so rotten; how I could think like that about my own woman. Forgive me, Sandeep."

"What's the point of apologizing now?" You and I have been pushed from the top. Have you been pretending for five years?" Sandeep said, irritated.

"No, Sandeep, there is no hypocrisy, only today I have made a mistake."

"One could make a mistake innocently. There is a difference between error and poison.

You must be thinking of another deal for Sweetie.

I understand everything. You guys are making excuses.

I have no value in this family. I have no right to decide anything. You don't love from the heart; this is your lust. Don't treat me like slut.."

Shera followed the same formula. He picked up the keys and left the house. That's how his tendency to go out of the house with his keys increased.

He became an alcoholic within months. Bibi always advises not to drink. He even mixed drinking and driving.

The daily grind increased even more, when Sandeep's parents also came.

It was also a day of fury for Shera when he broke another of his principles.

He was alone at home. Sandeep had gone on to her parent's basement, staying the night there, and Bibi had gone to someone's house in the morning to recite Sukhmani Sahib

Nowadays, whenever Shera was alone, he starts drinking. Sometimes he would fall asleep, and sometimes he would start kicking. He would talk to himself, and Sandeep and Bibi would listen to him.

Both were miserable, even though their reasons for being miserable were their own.

There was no one to listen to today.

"Why doesn't she understand me? I don't know; I don't get it.... Suddenly, his eyes fell on the corner of Sandeep's Diary under the top shelf of clothes.

No, no, he turned around and went downstairs. The fridge opened and closed.

Early in the morning, after taking scotch, He needed something to eat, but he opened and closed the fridge again and went upstairs. Put scotch and drank a lot and then another shot.

He was sleepy now.

He lay down on the bed and closed his eyes.

The corner of the Diary was spinning in his mind.

He got up and opened the Diary. At one point, Sandeep had said that Shera could read this Diary, he did not read it, and now he should not have read the Diary, but he got busy reading it.

As it was read, the forbidden fruit covered with leaves was exposed.

"He did not dare to read the entire Diary. He got up, looked at the bottle, and cursed himself. Why did I break my principle?

Her life can't affect me, but I have to control external waves. Where I become weak, I could not understand?

What is the difference between the two of us? Nothing you are the same, alcohol answered.

We are just hypocrites. Both Sandeep and I. Why am I interfering in someone's privacy? Am I a traditional husband too? Has a woman become a property for me also?

No, I'm wrong; I don't even have the right to live anymore.

Just then, Bibi said from inside him, 'Don't think like this. You are my darling son; I live for you; you are my world. Why don't you have the right to live?

I don't know, Bibi, my thinking power has lost its breath.

He got dizzy and went to the washroom, and started vomiting. Nothing was coming out from inside.

More alcohol was needed, but there was no more at home.

He dialed Sati's phone number with trembling hands.

"Satti, give me a bottle of liquor now, just now."

"But, the liquor store is not open yet."

"I don't care, break the lock of the liquor store." He hung up the phone.

"Bibi, you are also a woman. I hate you too."

About half an hour later, the doorbell rang. Shera opened the door, and Sati was standing outside, smiling.

He had a plastic bag in his hand. Shera grabbed the bag from Sati. He stopped Sati and tell him to leave. Sati saw him drunk and want to stay for help.

Shera said, "Now you go; I will call if needed."

Satti stood up for a while and then left.

Shera opened the half-filled bottle.

When Sandeep returned, Shera was fast asleep, and Bibi was sitting in the living room, worried.

"Come on, Sandeep, I want to talk to you."

"Yes, biji."

"Daughter, please solve your differences, save your family. Don't create negativity."

What's so significant about a goat's head?"

"Biji, look, there is nothing from my side. Let me make it simple. Don't want to marry Sweetie? If you have to, why can't you marry Sohan? Nowadays, everything works."

"Daughter, it doesn't happen in a relationship, but for your sake, Shera spoke to Sweetie. She refused. She is in love with someone and says that she has to marry him. Now you tell me how we can force her."

"But, Shera didn't tell me anything."

"What can he tell you now?"

Without answering, Sandeep went upstairs. He saw Shera asleep, two empty bottles, and her diary open.

Shera got up in the morning and did not talk to anybody, and went to work.

When he returned, he fell asleep and got up in the evening to get ready for the party. Nowadays, Sandeep did not go with him, and Shera stopped asking.

On the way, he got very thirsty and turned the car into a plaza. He took Sprite's can and got into the car. Turn left and head north again with the adjacent lights. As he turned, he went to the other side of the road. He stopped the car following the red lights.

Just then, a van stopped on the other side of the adjacent divider. He lost. He didn't care. He felt the van's windshield open, and the horn sounded again.

Now the green lights were gone. There was a left-turn light.

He did not walk because cars were coming from the other side. People were blowing horns. He had no idea why people were blowing their horns and watching at him.

He looked at the van. There was a Punjabi woman in it. He lowered the mirror and heard the woman's screams, "Look where you are standing." Now the horns were ringing for her too. People thought they were related, know each other.

One is upset, and the other is persuading him.

Van Driver brought her van to the intersection and signaled the people to stop. People stood in a daze, and Shera turned her car around. As he drove slowly to the right, he saw the van following him.

Shera slowed down so that the van could pass, but Van kept following him. There were a couple of turns, but Van did not leave him. By this time, the banquet hall had arrived, and Shera had parked the car.

When he parked the van, the woman turned the van around and left.

Shera closed his eyes. He was thinking, who was this lady—my bibi, Sandeep, or some other gender.

Who am I, driving the car. Maybe I am Sohan, and the Van driver was Sandeep.

Maybe She is Sati, a turning woman.

Maybe I lost and waiting for the next train.

DIVORCE PARTY

"**I**'M TIRED OF the daily grind. Why don't you get a divorce? Is this life worth living?" Simran sipped his beer and looked at the beer bottle, tearing its raised label.

"Yeah, bro, you're right; we have to do something," Preet replied.

"Why do you try to strike your foot on ax? Your home is currently worth around 1 million. If your mom and dad got divorced, it wouldn't be living at home, the two would be separated, and what would happen to your future? Their cousin Nihal, who had come to them in the afternoon, spoke

"Nihal, you don't know, they have built our life hell, they fight every day.

You know Preet and me, like Survival show, we just love the show. We wait for the front, and precisely at that time, they start exchanging hotshots. When they fight, we can't enjoy our show. We told them so many times, don't fight between ten and eleven but never listen. They also start in front of our guests.

A few days ago, Dad brought Mickey. He wants to adjust and start buying Micky instead of a bottle. He also drank in the washroom so that mom won't see him. Mom is a genius. Mom finds out after the third peg, that's all. Dad picked up the car in protest and went and fetched the whole pitcher.

We were scared but baffled they came out of the bedroom in the morning laughing beautifully. Dude, we get confused; what are they doing, and how do they get along? Is? They enter the bedroom as if only one would come out alive now.

In the morning, they take tea, breakfast, and they go back to work. If fight, smile, go shopping, celebrate Diwali, why they are confusing us."

"What's so significant about a fight?" Nihal asked.

"They need something little to fight for, they think bored of each other, are not living life, we're just spending our days, and we want that they both should live their life nicely with their taste. They should not interfere with each other personal life.

Dad loves to drink, but Mom hates this habit. Mom uses to go to her friend's home to listen to a saint's narration, but Dad does not like it. Dad said that the saint is a hypocrite, a womanizer, and a thug.

Mom does not want to listen against her Guru. Dad said if you wish to religious teachings, go to Gurdwara, a traditional way. Both love their lifestyles. So we want them to get a divorce." Simran said.

"Preet, what about more beer. Do we have more, or that's it? Seems like three more left, and it is not even six o'clock yet."

"Nihal Veere, we don't have more, yes. Dad has it, but he will not give it to us for free. I have to pay Dad's sixty dollars, and Simran has to pay in hundreds, so, you ask and see." You will probably get it for free."

"Preet, why don't you do this? Ask Mom for money and get beer from Dad with the same money." Simran devised a plan.

"I ask and see, but what excuse should I make?"

"Say you want to get a memory card."

"Yes, that's right."

Preet got up from the yard and went inside to the kitchen. Mom took out her purse; there was no money in it, then she took out Joginder Singh's wallet from his pant.

She took out a fifty-dollar note and gave it to Preet, saying, go quickly, today is Saturday, the Mall will not be closed, you have almost one hour only."

"OK, Mom, I'm leaving now."

Preet then went to the yard and showed the note and said, "Done job."

"Nihal, now you go to Dad. He has a case of 24 Canadian beer. He has kept it for guests only.

He doesn't drink beer. Hold the dollar in your hand so that Dad doesn't give up."

Nihal went inside and climbed the stairs. Joginder Singh was reading a book in his room. Seeing Nihal, he put the book aside."

"Fuffer Ji, I want a favor from you; we need a beer case but don't want to go outside. Simran told me you have a beer box. Please take cost, and You'll get more tomorrow."

"No, I have not opened a liquor store here. Did you see a sign outside my room, `Cold beer sold here!'"

"Hey, hey, weekend, just relax."

"OK, I'll give it to you, but I have a condition."

"What's that, uncle?"

"Don't call me fuffar; tell me fuffarh in Punjabi once."

"I have tried many times, but I can't just accent problem."

Joginder Singh laughed and said, take the beer, ask Simran to take it from the cold room, and also show me this fifty dollars note; it looks like mine."

"No, uncle, I got it out of the ATM yesterday."

"Look, Preet is your sister; stop her from drinking beer. In our culture, our girls don't drink."

"Fuffer ji, we'll talk to her, but she drinks only for when she in our company, not much."

"Go well now; you will be waiting, and tell your aunt to come and listen to me."

Saying goodbye, Nihal came down.

Nihal gave the fifty dollar note to Preet, Preet gave it to Mom, and Mom again put it in Joginder Singh's pocket.

"Then, when to talk about divorce with Mom and Dad?" Simran started talking again.

"It only came to our notice now. The plan should be such that they do not even start hating each other. They should be separate, like friends.

Sometimes they fight and talk about divorce, but relatives start explaining their duties and tell them to think about kids. Then they became wise again, think about our future and start loving each other.

"Nihal, your mother played a big role in this. You should tell your mother don't poke her nose too much in our family matters." Simran said.

"Yes, bro, let's start with your mother first. Does she suck your father's blood too?" Preet also entered the discussion.

"Yes, that's right, I will talk to my mom too. She should not interfere with your family matters." Nihal wants to be impartial.

"Your mother is the root cause of every problem. She has nothing to do after making two chapatis" Preet also supported Simran.

"Guys ... Guys, my mom, and dad are not in such a bad condition, and let's finish something first. We are talking about your parents here."

"I say marriage should not be a rope when there is tension, separate. Do we need to interfere in each other's affairs?"

Now tell me, guys, when was the biggest fight? Has the police ever been involved?"

"About ten years ago, once the police came but returned empty-handed with shame. Preet was in seventh grade, and I was in ninth grade."

"What happened?" Nihal asked.

"Not to mention, but if you have to ask, your mom came, she was the one who set the trap." At first, they kept grumbling inside; we understood that it was a serious matter.

Then your mother started talking loudly and after put on her shoes and went out. Mom, Dad also went out. Hearing the noise on the road, the neighbor called the police. Your mother left, and the police came to our house." Simran became silent after speaking, and Preet said, "Mom, Dad told the whole story to the police."

"Come on, kids, come in; there's a mosquito out there now." Mahinder Kaur called out to the children.

The three went inside. Joginder Singh was watching TV in the living room. Preet went to the kitchen with Mom, and Nihal and Simran sat in the living room. The youth had intoxication in their eyes, and they were in the mood to talk to Joginder Singh today. At first, Nihal said, "Fufar ji, tell me what marriage means, why to get married?"

"Strange question, didn't your dad ever tell you?"

"Fuffer, don't associate the matter with an accent. Don't cut short with fun. We are not kids anymore, answer directly."

Marriage does not mean a lifelong honeymoon Nihal. There are some responsibilities, and to fulfilling those responsibilities, there are sometimes different views.

For the last twenty-seven years, I have not explained to your aunt that there are no ghosts, just blind faith from some mischievous people. She never believes me.

There are many other things where we don't get along, and sometimes there is bitterness in nature, but that doesn't mean we should separate?"

By now, Preet and Mohinder Kaur had also come into the living room and started listening to them.

"You should understand the meaning of possessiveness; why do you want your wife to think the way you do?"

"This is my wife; how can I want to hurt her? What is right is right. What is wrong is wrong. Now your aunt goes to hear a story from a thief."

"Beware, if you called our Baba a thug. He is not a cheater. He explained the way to God."

Mohinder Kaur spoke angrily.

"Happy to see your aunt? my wife, who can't even know how to speak with her husband."

"Sardar Ji, you drink alcohol every day. How good is that? If I listen to Baba Ji's discourse, why do you feel dizzy?"

"Your Baba has only come to collect money, yes or no?"

"For God's sake, don't burden yourself. The blessing has already flown from our home. Baba ji wants to pile up Maya(money) in the blink of an eye, but he is not miraculous."

"It's all over again, Dad ... Mom ... Please live the rest of your life happily; if you can't live in peace, then why don't you divorce each other?" Simran said a little angrily.

"Yes, of course, Simran, you are right," Nihal spoke.

"That's what we were going to talk to you about today. "Preet broke the whole pot.

"All three of you should just leave our home. Come on, get on your shoes, or pick your shoes and leave home. You should wear your shoes on the road. Nihal, get out of my home and take them with you. Otherwise, you know my nature." Joginder Singh growled, and the three children got up to go. They knew Dad's orders. On such occasions, the matter was bound to escalate, no matter where it started, at the end, it would finish on Mohinder Kaur.

"Please let them eat and drink." Mohinder Kaur said.

"Do whatever you have to do but leave the living room." With that, Joginder Singh himself got up and went upstairs.

The whole house fell silent. The three of them ate quietly and left the place to go to Nihal. After they left, Mohinder Kaur also went upstairs, went to Joginder Singh's room, and said, "Sometimes you even cross the limit. Why did the children be treated like that?

What would your sister think?"

"Look, Mona, these kids are going crazy every day; this is not a way to talk to your parents.

Why not get a divorce?"

"you are right, Sardar Ji; the mouths of the children are broken nowadays. Do they know what difficulties we have built the house? Until midnight you kept delivering pizzas to people in the snow. What is the special wish of the children that we have not fulfilled? But what can be done now that this has already happened?"

"I have to think something, Mona. I'm not angry at all. You understand, and I understand. Our fight has never gone out of the wall. People have gone to court every third day."

"But we didn't realize that even the people living inside the walls would become our enemies. The race born here thinks we are monkeys. Don't have fun.

We should have fun or build a house?"

"Come on, don't put it on your heart, take a peg if you want to, and then go to bed." These trifles are part of life, don't you care too much,

I will take a shower and fresh myself. It is not bad anyway; two weeks passed, we did not have time like this."

"Yes, the best time for romance, dear. Don't take a shower. You are good to me just like that."

"Let me go, Sardar Ji. You need a special romance today." Mohinder went to the washroom with a smile.

"Why do people get divorced, Moninder?

"Nowadays divorce parties are also taking place. Long articles are being written about it. It is said to be comfortably separated by love and celebrated. Simran was saying that he has a friend; his parents had a divorce party and then split like friends; I found it very strange." Mohinder said while brushing her washed hair.

"I don't understand what kind of friendship a man and a woman have? What if the couple later became friends?"

"You're starting to taste it; that's something to think about."

"Let's get a divorce, there will be a party under this pretext.

The children will be happy, we will be alone, and we will meet secretly, like Romeo Juliet; what do you think?" Mohinder said affectionately.

"Why, didn't your Baba give you this advice?"

"How many times have you been told not to mix cannabis with a good time, especially when we are in bed? Why do you bring Baba Ji in?"

"Baba doesn't come if you don't push me on my peg all the time; I'm not a fool; what if someone got tired and took a peg or two."

"No, you don't stay on one or two pegs. Even today, your children are angry. What was the need to speak loudly? I am thinking about my sister now. What will she say about it?

"Don't worry; she is my sister. she knows me."

"Let's talk about the divorce party?" Mohinder said.

"Even at these parties, everything is the same as the celebration party; the shame is removed.

The cake is cut, the wedding ring is returned, the banner of 'Just Divorce' is put up, sometimes the divorce ring is also worn. this ring is in the shape of a broken circle."

"How interesting, Jazzy?"

"It is lovely.

"why don't you call me 'Jazzy' in public, you say so nicely. I feel we just married. How romantically you call me Jazzy?"

"I'm ashamed."

"And not ashamed in the bedroom?"

"Don't say so; you know what I mean in the bedroom."

"Tell me something today before I tell you further?"

"Yes, please?" Mohinder said playfully.

"When Nihal did such a bad thing, I once thought that they have to leave the house today. I found a big excuse for our lovemaking. It's been two weeks, let's meet."

"How smart you are. Children must be thinking; we have been fighting, and we ..."

"It's called an adjustment. If the kids don't understand our problems, then we have to make our schemes."

"Why not stop fighting in front of them?"

"It's OK; this is our home. We could fight at any time. We can fight when we have time, but you are also right. They grow up now. We should avoid chirping sound."

"Mona honey, Let's talk about the divorce party. You know better than me because kids told you everything."

"This party is done jointly by both of them. Sometimes they shared the cost, but sometimes one person spends. It's not just fun; sometimes it's emotional.

Emotional, heartfelt words use to express their pain and apologize to others. Efforts are made to keep friends and relatives comfortable. Try to reduce the bitterness of divorce.

The reasons for the failure of marriage is being told.

It is said that there is a difference in our views and it is not possible to live together anymore.

"Mona Honey, do you think that such dramatic actions could diminish hate?"

"Jazzy darling, that's the difference. We associate separation with hate; maybe there are other reasons too.

They say, 'What's the point of living together if you feel boredom in your partner's company.

"Honey, I don't understand?" I was reading a report on the subject. The number of parties is increasing, and their popularity is reaching an all-time high. It is an attempt to lighten the dissolved stigma of the institution of marriage. Books are being written on how to have a divorce party."

"Let go of me and tell the children not to run away; this is not our time. Do what you have to do with me."

"Just leave the topic Jazzy, I just want from you. Don't argue with kids. It is not our time. If you are upset, call me and say whatever you feel. I understand you by heart, but kids not."

"As you order Honey, sometimes it doesn't make sense, anything comes out of the mouth in a hurry, and I am not their enemy?" I understand everything, but what to do now? Everything will be fine, Simran is on the job, Preet will be on, and we will be free and safe."

"Turn off the lights; it's past midnight with the divorce party." Let's have a wedding party now." Joginder Singh said and turned his face toward Mohinder for a kiss.

At ten o'clock in the morning, the doorbell rang, and Mohinder put on her sleeper and opened the door. There were kids outside.

"Good morning Bhuya Ji, we have come to eat potato paranthas." Saying this, the three came inside.

"Didn't you have a phone call before?" I have no preparation. The flour is yet to be Knead; the potatoes are to be boiled, the hour will pass quickly."

"Mom, I'll help you." You take the flour, and I boil the potatoes." Preet said.

"Did Dad wake up?" Simran asked.

"No, he is still in bed; I'll make tea for him first."

"I have to apologize to my uncle; I told my mother the whole thing; she was furious, saying you don't know how to talk to adults."

After listening to him for so long, Joginder Singh also came down the stairs and said, "Good morning, guys."

"Good morning," the three almost said together.

"Sorry fufferji, for last night."

"That's OK, Nihal, but how did you come to think of it? We spent the night thinking about it. The whole night passed in thoughts."

"Flatly, it is our mistake; it simply came to our notice then. We want you to be happy, together or separated; you know we both love both of you."

"Your thinking is good, but it doesn't match our thinking. For us, marriage is not just our happiness; it is a family."

"Just stop it now, don't talk about it anymore, you would be upset again, I know you. Come on, Nihal and Simran, come here and peel the onions if you want to eat." Mahinder Kaur roared from the kitchen.

"Let me talk, Mohinder, I listen to them, yes guys, tell me your story, what do you mean about your happiness? Maybe we can learn something from you."

"No, please send the children to the kitchen to me. You can rest for an hour. You haven't slept all night, and you haven't let me sleep," Mohinder roared from the kitchen.

"Dad, Nihal will explain, he knows how to tell, but promise, you won't be upset."

"OK, I don't mind," Joginder said, holding a cup of tea from Mohinder.

"Fuffer ji, the thing is that marriage is a combination of two genders, they decide to live together. It is not necessary to get married, life can be started without marriage. As long as they can create happiness for each other, but if the relationship is not going well, what is the harm in separation? That's all there is to it."

"How do you know our relationship is not going well? It's not a relationship if I don't sleep and your aunt doesn't sleep either. This is called being a partner of sorrow and happiness; what is another relationship?" Joginder Singh looked at Mohinder as she was leaving and said hurriedly.

"Don't you think that individual happiness is what it means? Is it seen only with physical pleasure?"

"No, there's no point in having sex only; it's like living together as friends. If you say so, I will take you to a divorce party. The last Saturday of this month is my friend's aunt's divorce party, the invitation is for me alone, but I will ask for you. He will not refuse."

"I have to go too," Mohinder said.

"I too," Preet also said.

"OK, I ask for everyone; I'll call now."

Nihal picked up the phone and called his friend. After talking for a while, he hung up the phone and said, "OK guys, get ready, we'll all go." We'll talk about the rest later; why not?"

"Yes, Nihal, we will all go to the party with you."

On the last Saturday of the month, they were all ready and waiting for Nihal, and at precisely six o'clock, Nihal came, and they went to Ramba Banquet Hall.

Outside the hall, snacks, and coffee, tea was provided, different groups had snacks. As if they had come for a happy occasion, the well-dressed people did not care if it was a wedding party or a divorce party. After having a snack, Nihal took everyone inside. Sitting at the reserved table, Nihal set out to find his friend. It seemed that he had not yet arrived.

Joginder Singh looked around. It was a fantastic atmosphere.

There were four divorce party flags. There were two tables on the side where people brought bouquets.

Their Bouquet was still on their table. Nihal wanted his friend to come so he could meet his aunt. Half the hall was full of guests, but people were still coming. At each table was a card for today's program schedule.

Joginder Singh opened the card and then closed it and walked towards the bar. He brought a peg of Scotch for himself and came to the table to read the card.

Above was written, Thank You For Coming, On Our Divorce Party, Ring-Off Ceremony. The program was drawn below. First, the best friend's speech, after that the cake will be cut, then there will be a ring off ceremony and then today's special couple will have their ideas. Joginder Singh read and smiled and handed the card to Mohinder. She was still reading when Nihal came to the table with his friend. After wishing them, he said, "Let me introduce you to my aunt."

Scindia, who was going to be Miss from Mrs., was wearing a light blue dress with a necklace of white pearls around her neck and ear tops of the same shade.

Joginder gazed at her deep low cut and presented her Bouquet.

Scindia accepted the flowers with a smile and said, "Let me introduce you to my ex-husband." Mr. Dominic was only two steps away. Dominic was also in full swing and welcomed the whole family.

After filling the food, everyone came to the table. Simran Nihal and Preet got up and went outside and said they would come back in five minutes.

"Where have they gone now?" Mohinder asked.

"I don't know. Am I an astrologer?"

"Just call and ask your Baba Ji; maybe he knows."

"Did you start again?" How many times have I told you not to talk about our Baba Ji."

A voice came from the stage, "Attention, please, friends, today's proceedings are about to begin; please sit down in your seats." Smirk for a few minutes, and everyone sat down in their seats.

The voice came from the stage again, "Friends, first of all, Mr. Joseph will address you and tell you about today's opportunity.

Madame Starry will tell you the past on her own, some other speakers, and if anyone has something to say, write on slip and give it to me." After that the cake will be cut, there will be a ring off ceremony and the last tango, that's all, the rest will be announced later.

Announcer Jimmy said, "Mr. Joseph, please come to the dice."

Joseph picked up the microphone, and everyone applauded.

"No couple gets married just because they get divorced tomorrow. But statistics show that many marriages end in divorce. Vows are taken at the time of marriage and vow to feed us around the religions. I ask why those who love take swear? In sorrow, in happiness, in sickness, in health, he may be a benefactor.

That one may not be able to bear one's illness; it may be that it may be a mental complication or a way of thinking! If you sit down and decide that it is difficult, then the divorce will be a logical step. What is the use of fighting every day? Is it better to separate and live your own life?

Yes, sometimes the situation becomes such that most people think that divorce is a good step. When one of the two, whether husband or wife, starts hating the other, hurts emotionally, finds excuses to insult the other, terrorizes the home, spreads the threat of mental violence, and so on. If such evil thoughts are born, it does rot; it does not remain hidden from others.

Don't you think that two bodies cannot be joined together with traditional glue? The combination of which then demands fragrance. Life is like a waterfall; God did not give us the energy to be ruined. I'm not saying there shouldn't be counseling to save a marriage. I am not saying that breaking up a wedding is a good thing. Although our culture doesn't allow it, it can't be made dirty." Joseph paused, took a glass of water from the table next to the dice, and drank.

Joseph grabbed the mic again and said, "Sometimes divorce is the only option left. Both for yourself and your partner. Our mission is to become friends and live each other's lives instead of parting with hatred if the partners can't stay. That's how the concept of 'live and let live' can be maintained; thank you, friends."

Joseph put the mic on the dice and walked to his table where a lovely girl was waiting for him. He was aware of every part of his limbs and did his best to show every limb. She looked like her daughter from a young age, but her sexy look, dress, and way of receiving Joseph back made her look like she couldn't be his daughter.

Joginder Singh looked at Mohinder and asked, "Do you understand?"

"Yes," Mohinder replied shortly.

She was looking at Joseph's table, and she said to Joginder about the girl's movements, ?"

"That is the reason I told you, don't fight with me. I am a very nice husband."

"I think they look like man and woman."

"let's ask Joseph?"

"Don't guess anything. I don't believe you; you could go to Joseph. Let's ask Nihal, but where are the three?

Mohinder looked around, and the three of them were standing in a corner talking. Mohinder signaled, and they walked towards the table. Mohinder stared into the hall. Everyone seemed happy. There was no sadness even though she thought that someone's house was falling apart

Simran Preet and Nihal came and sat on the chairs around the table.

"Nihal, do you know about the girl sitting next to Joseph?"

"Why, fuffarji, do you want to be friends?" Nihal said with a laugh.

"Let me save your aunt, that's enough; what else do I have to do? I have just asked to calm down my curiosity."

"She's a receptionist at Joseph's real estate office. Joseph is a broker and a big businessman. Real estate dollars have not been enough for him, and now he is trying his luck in the stock market."

"But why didn't his wife come along?" Mohinder asked.

"He doesn't have a wife; he's alone."

"Why not get married?"

"Bhuya ji got it done, but it didn't work out. She took half of the property and separated last year."

"Now, this girl will take the other half."

"Dad, why do you think that? Whatever he does, who cares?"

"Nyla is Joseph's girlfriend. Joseph Just afforded Her, That's All. How do you like Joseph's ideas, Fufferji?"

"OK, one side, I don't agree with him."

"Would you like to share your thoughts with everyone? Language is no barrier; I will interpret."

"Yeah yeah ... yeah, I'd like to talk too. Will give me time?"

"Let me ask?" Nihal got up and left.

After a while, Nihal came back and said, "Yes, Fufer Ji, another one has to speak before you, then your turn." Time-up in ten minutes."

Mike's voice came from the stage again. "Friends, you heard Joseph's thoughts. If you have any questions, write them down." Now Mr. Butler will give his views, his time is ten minutes, and after that, Mr. Joginder will speak for ten minutes. Write down any questions you have about the speaker and send them to the person concerned, who will answer them later or to me. And now Mr. Butler, welcome to the dice, please!"

"Friends, you heard Joseph's thoughts. I have to deliver the same thing, but my point of view is a bit different. Same Chicken with Different Spice - Butler paused for a minute and looked around as if guessing whether people were paying attention or not. He was satisfied that the eyes of the people were on him. He nodded a little and said, "A woman and a man have assessed each other's strengths in bed, so there is no illusion, but when there is a rift, the matter does not remain." They can't sleep like before. A woman and a man who are husband and wife and are not happy with this relationship feel physically threatened by each other. In this situation, there are two possibilities.

On the one hand, they cannot enjoy, and on the other, they are afraid of life; they do not know how much poison there is in the other. Many conservative families force them to live in danger. Sometimes in the name of God, sometimes in the name of values. Isn't that cruel?

These are three types of hidden crimes. The first crime is that everyone is free; they cannot be forced to be in danger. The second crime is social. By saving such an unhappy marriage, we are committing a social crime. The third God, for the sake of God, saved marriage, also deletes our devotion to God, so the only solution to a sick marriage is to end it. In the civilization we are living in today, there is no room for anyone to pose. All are free who cannot respect the other's freedom and has no right to be with them. This is how we will destroy our future generations.

There is another problem in such marriages; it is a betrayal of this institution. Even those who believe in this institution should not forget its sanctity; times have changed and are changing. It is also essential for some couples to separate for the sanctity of marriage and maintain the sanctity of life by marrying another like-minded person. Feelings of distrust, betrayal in a relationship, marriage is nothing more than a night bar. Sometimes this crime becomes so severe that it cannot be forgiven. What is the need to forgive? When we have other ways. Let's congratulate Scindia and Dominic today, celebrate the beginning of a new life, and enjoy society's health. Thank you." Butler stepped back with applauding.

Harry grabbed the mic and said, "Friends, I have learned that Mr. Joginder Singh is a staunch supporter of the marriage institution.

He is against divorce and the divorce party. We want their views to listen carefully, but there must be a gap between the two different perspectives. We do not become passive about any one idea, and this balance is maintained. Let's take a ten-minute break after Starry.

Please discuss with those sitting at the table next to us, after which we will listen to Madam Starry's Personal life and opinion. After that, Joginder Singh will have his views. Enjoy yourself."

Starry, began to speak as if she were in a hurry to speak her mind.

"I have two sons and a daughter and I have been married for twenty-two years.

I was living my life when suddenly one day I found a friend from my school. I had no intention of establishing a relationship with him, but I don't know why my heart became restless. It seemed like I fell in love with him after so many years.

Many questions blocked my way. I remembered everything I had experienced in the past. When I got married, I had kids, the kids started going to school, and I wasted years of my life just for them. Never think about myself.

Mechanically, I slept with my husband at night. Gradually, I realized that I didn't even love my hubby. I had no romance with him, no intensity, no urgency. In all my interests, he was nowhere to be seen. I began to wonder why I was living such a boring life; it was a sick married relationship that I was carrying.

In fact, the perfect man for me had just arrived, my schoolmate—the mischief with Michael, the talk of the town, and the urge for coffee. While sipping coffee, I remembered that I had once shared a cup of coffee with Michael.

One day after finishing the coffee, I thought different. Is this stupid, what I am thinking?

Life is done now; it's over, nothing left behind. These dreams no longer matter. I came back home. The next morning I took a shower and went to my office feeling miserable. Everyone in the office was looking happy, fresh faces, my colleagues walking around. When someone walked with someone and someone with someone, I was sitting alone in my cabin.

When it was put in the filter, Gathering the thoughts felt that a spark was burning. It was clear that the spark was burning. The wave in my body was like a wave that had become negative in me. I went to the washroom, and through the mirror, I saw myself young.

Starry paused and breathed. Her breathing seemed as if her decision was still incomplete. "The choice is there, Starry and Starry with family. The family, which is busy, have no time for Starry.

"What do you think, Mohinder, what will be her next story?"

"Yeah, crazy, I don't know what will happen, the old woman is on fire; what else is the loss of shame?"

They were whispering that Starry started talking again. There was no interest in the children. They were sipping beer and talking to each other and probably talking about a TV show.

"Why the change? It's something to think.

I think it must have been God's will. He was performing miracles just to make me happy. It is also HIS duty; we are all HIS children; HE has to follow as well; of course, in my case, HE made a mistake which he wanted to correct. Otherwise, what was the need to send Dominic back into my life? My dilemma became even more vital when I found out that Dominic is single nowadays. His two daughters lived with their boyfriends,

His wife was living in a relationship with someone other than him and was now alone.

Sometimes I even think I'm wrong.

Sometimes I get sick, but Dominic forbade me to sin. Last Christmas,

I finally revealed the secret of my heart. I married Dominic, and to be honest, I have never looked back, and now I am thrilled. Lately, I have finally found the love of my peers."

"I wish I could get my first love 'Sunil' too, without wasting a minute, I would have married her."

"Yes, Jazzy, I'm ready to be a mediator, but her husband is six feet tall."

"That's the noise, the real problem. Otherwise, I could do the same thing. You know I still have a spark."

Joginder said, "Why are you so quiet, Mona."

"I am thinking Jazzy, which one I choose? There are so many."

Starry's voice echoed again, "What a beautiful life you have when you don't have to make any sacrifices for your dreams." Silent and sad, Starry didn't know if she was happy or in a dilemma, but her next thing shook everyone according to their thinking.

She was saying, "Friends, what a life that is when you get everything you once wished for and prayed for."

Dreaming is life, and when it is achieved without any hesitation. It is like the grace of God. That dream, about which you have to work very hard, also teaches you many lessons. You are the hero of life if you can find real happiness in life even after spending a lot of experience. Today I am happy and wish everyone in the world happiness. Being possessive is a disease. I just do and wish all the best for the decision to let two people live life in their way today. Rejoice forever."

Starry placed the mic on the table and walked to her table to Applause.

The whole hall was abuzz again. People were coming to the bar for snacks, coffee, and tea.

"Mohinder this is what happens in rituals. This impossible thing happens in us; when it happens, we are broken, we keep on squirming all our lives, and we spend our lives cursing ourselves. In North America, just like marriage, divorce is a method they have built. It has different purposes. They have made divorce a celebration, just like marriage.

"You're right, Jazzy."

"Fufferji, now it's your turn, think about what to say. Don't Let's down."

"I want to drink a peg. Then I will take another double; after all, I have to tell the truth."

Mohinder went to the washroom, and the kids went outside. Joginder was alone on the table, and after taking double, he was drunk. He was talking to Mohinder while she was not there.

"It only came to our notice then. I can't believe it."

"That is not Simran; I have not shied away. These are all lost people; they have to be told what marriage is, understand?"

Then he heard the voice of Preet," Nihal, go and cut Dad's name and come."

"No, Nihal, you swear, I will speak today."

"Fuffer ji, tell me first what you will say, just give me a few points." It will be easier for me to start interpreting."

"I think about it; I also consult your aunt."

"Yes, yes, Dad, go there and open the helpline, call India."

"Simran No, no, it is not a joke; listen to your dad today. What do they say, yes, philosophy?

Three kids came back; they heard Dad's whisper. Mohinder came back too. She was upset.

"Nihal, let's go out; I'm suffocating here." The three of them got up and walked out."

On the way, Nihal called Joseph and cut off Joginder Singh's name.

"Listen, Friends; I've come to your meeting today with my point. If it seems right, then accept it. Otherwise, I am not just saying but living what I say.

Marriages are settled in heaven; there is the only celebration on earth.

Some believe in it, and some deny it. Denial does not change the truth. Yeah, Al, that sounds pretty crap to me.

The rest of your physical deeds are to be decided by God and not by you. It seems to me that everyone in this crowd is sitting away from God.

Our culture says this, One saint in India narrate in one gathering that one day a man leaves his father and mother and goes to his wife, and their two bodies become one and create the new light.

When creating a new one, they are not two but one. If God has made them one, then who are we to separate them into two?

When two bodies are on the path of creation as one, then they are one body, then the question of separation does not arise. It is a matter of turning away from God. Science has not yet advanced enough to operate on one body to connect half of its body to another's body."

Mohinder broke the chain of Joginder Singh's thoughts by speaking. "What are you muttering?" How many times have you been told to look for an opportunity? I will not let you say, in front of everyone, these people will not understand what is in your heart."

The children had returned, and Joginder sat on a chair, totally drunk.

He was looking at them. Nihal Singh smiled and said, "let's go home, Fufferji."

"No, I have to go on stage, it is my turn now."

"Let it be, Fulfer Ji, don't make such a fuss." Think about it, you mild-mannered man."

"Nihal, don't worry, they won't talk. Nothing went wrong; I know your Fuffarji," Mohinder said.

Mohinder was smiling. Today was her day. Joginder Singh may or may not speak, but he was happy today. She looked lovingly at Joginder Singh, waving a spoon into tea and saying, "Yes, you are very wise. If you just learn to be quiet, there is no one else like you."

"Mohinder, I know you think so. Even in your fight, there is warmth, but the children do not understand." "Ask them."

"To whom?"

"To all those who are gathered here, including kids, what is home? Can't the person in the house even raise his voice by shouting?"

"Why not?" You have never been like this. Before marriage, and even after ten years of marriage, you did not even touch alcohol."

Joginder Singh's eyes widened. He picked up his leftover glass emotionally and put it to his mouth but did not drink and then put it on the table. He looked at Mohinder once and smiled, and then closed his eyes.

"Friends, you can ask my wife; she is sitting at the table in a green suit. I did not drink alcohol. By the time I was 35, I was a teetotaler. Suddenly one day in a gathering, without thinking, I picked up a glass of liquor from my friend sitting next to me and drank it in one gulp. Alcohol ripped through my chest and spread throughout my body.

Everyone was as surprised as you are today, yet I have to tell you the truth. Mahinder Kaur is sitting with me now.

I don't know if she had emotional feelings for someone who just obeyed her family and married me. Today, twenty-seven years have passed, not a single happiness I gave her. Fights and fights but never thought of separating from each other."

The hall resounded with Applause. When the Applause subsided, Joginder Singh's voice echoed in the hall. Sitting at the table, Joginder Singh wanted to see the people around him clapping, but perhaps they had stopped clapping; he closed his eyes again.

"You don't know what Wari suits are, and I didn't come to tell you about Wari suits in ten minutes. All I can say is that the basement moisture ruined them. We were looking for a new place in the snow when Mohinder's fingers froze.

Don't worry; she got better, she told me quickly. Otherwise, she has a habit of not speaking until she faints. I brought her back to the basement, soaked her fingers in hot water, and broke the freeze. That day was our most beautiful day. The Goddess of Beauty descended from time to time.

I heard something from the sky; why it was happening, I don't know who it was, I don't know. There was only one star. There was no Mohinder Kaur and no Joginder Singh.

Blood began to run in the frozen fingers; one finger began to caress my hair, the pollen was flying, butterflies were hovering, flying from one branch to another

, Who has been able to stop the flying butterflies to date? Will you destroy the butterflies from flying because of this function? I respect your point, but I can't entirely agree with it."

"Please don't drink anymore. I have hidden half your bottle at home. Drink at home if you need it." Mohinder said to mutter Joginder.

"But Mohinder, it's not my turn yet. I have to give a lecture; then I have to answer people's questions. What's the hurry? Tomorrow is Sunday; what work are we going to do?"

"Jazzy, If you obey me, I will reward you."

"Fufferji, have you thought about what to say?"

"Yes, divorce is killing the United States, Canada, and the church. Broken promises, distrust, instability, is another word you people can't understand."

"What's that, uncle?"

"Fragmentation"

"Dad, we know you're philosophical smart, but being smart isn't enough these days." Simran, who had been silent for a long time, broke his silence.

"But Dad doesn't understand a thing. You said divorce is killing the United States, Canada, and the church." I can't understand this. How can that be?"

"Preet, these are the things we need to understand, whether they are Indians like Canadians or me like you. Divorce is a national disaster, a hidden enemy that we do not understand."

Marriage is not a caste experience that doesn't matter if it fails; it has a lot to do with it. If we say the whole society and the entire country are connected, then there will be no exaggeration. It's a festival, and the celebration never goes away, guys."

"No, Dad, you're just trying to force your caste ideas. It's not going to be a workout, so just relax."

"I am relaxed., those who walk around are not relaxed. Marriage is a sacred bond, a woman's fulfillment, and a man's union with God through his wife."

"Dad, then why are you fighting with Mom so hard?" Preet asked.

"My fight has nothing to do with it. When do I say I'm perfect?" You guys couldn't understand the world I inherited."

"Just a minute Dad."

Divorcing couple came to greet them and accept their presence." "Hi Guys, we are honored with your presence. Please accept our thanks."

"Hi friends, good for you," Nihal said to Scindia and Dominic.

"Uncle, are you enjoying it?" Scindia called Joginder the head of the table.

"Yes," Joginder Singh replied shortly.

"Are you giving your opinion?" Scindia asked the second question.

"I Don't Think So!" Simran said.

"Why not?"

"Because my dad is not feeling well."

"It simply came to our notice now. Enjoy yourself." With that, they both went to the next table.

Joginder was feeling humiliated. He slowly got up, took another double peg from the bar, and followed his footsteps back to his table.

After he left, Simran said to Mom, "Mom, what do you think, Dad will be fine?" Otherwise, let's go home? We don't want Dad to create a scene."

"Son, I've known your dad for twenty-seven years. It never happened. They love you so much; nothing will embarrass you. Don't think that he fights with me. He never fights; his only way to protest is what I understand; you can't understand the depth of that way."

Joginder came back, and Simran said, "Good Mom, take care, we are around."

They left in silence.

"What did you say?" Joginder asked.

"Nothing."

"I understand everything. The thing was happening to me, I know. When you are talking to your kids, my back was watching you. Sometimes you become too much wax."

"Did I talk to the children and ask you something?"

"No"

"Why do you always feel right about everything?"

A peg of Scotch piercing inside, Joginder Singh was shaken; this shake was also his thinking. He put a poisonous smile on his face and calmed down again. He shook his head a couple of times and said, "I just hate divorce."

Mahinder Kaur knew why he was saying that but remained silent.

"Your attention please, a voice came from the stage. The whole hall was shaken.

Scindia and Dominic have welcomed you all. There will be a Ring off Ceremony, followed by Scindia and Dominic's Last Slow Dance." Applause resounded throughout the hall.

Scindia and Dominic took each other's hands and came to the bottom of the stage. They hugged each other. Dominic kissed Scindia's forehead and grabbed the mic and said, "I still love you, Scindia, but, unfortunately, I'm not with you anymore."

The two years I have spent with you are the treasure of my whole life. I will never forget that in my entire life. During my illness, when I had only the hospital walls, you made those walls paradise. I was worried day and night. All the loss that is to be separated from you is mine. I pray that wherever you are, be happy, and God will always have a merciful hand on your head, and I am sure that will be the case. God bless you. Thank you for spending two years with me, IM's loser.

Now it was Scindia's turn, "So sweet Dominic, these last words of yours are a testament to the love you gave me." I felt such feelings for the second time. My dad always took care of me, just like that. My minute by minute news, my smallest happiness, became a mission for him.

I was seventeen years old, and I didn't have any boyfriend, and the biggest concern was my dad. Whatever, wherever he could, he would try to surround me with a handsome boy and bring him to me. I would get angry, it was my contempt, my inner woman, but Dad didn't understand. Today, I confess in front of everyone that when my father died, I was relieved somewhere. I was crying, but my heart said that everyone is acceptable to go; Dad is gone. Now I can live my life. I loved Dad very much, but I could not bear him over protection. After he left and after your marriage, you started doing the same thing, my dear Dominic.

Fear was born while Living with you. It was as if Dad had been born again. This fear and its shadow will swallow me. I tried to associate with you many times, but you could not understand my need. Dominic, you are perfect, you will get a better girl than me, you deserve it too, she will be fortunate, but she is not me. I don't want anyone to control me like my dad. May you be happy wherever you are. I am leaving this city. I'd like to see you again, as a friend, maybe five or seven years later. I'm sure you'll set yourself up by then.

"Dear Dominic, Be sure to ask the new girlfriend before the wedding if she wants to be in control. Don't lose heart; many want to be in control. You'll find someone nice, chubby; wish you all the best, Dominic, and thank you, friends."

Jimmy grabbed Scindia and Dominic and said, "All right folks, now let's enjoy." First, there will be a slow dance of Scindia and Dominic, then a slow one for all of us, a very slow hahaha, and finally a tango."

"Oh yes, come on, guys."

"Dominic grabbed Scindia's hand and led her to the floor, kissed her hand, and they started dancing." There was a sudden silence. The lights went out. After the dance was over, they came to their table holding hands."

People were walking around, talking and walking to some bars, everyone knew that after the Ring off Ceremony, there would be a floor dance."

Suddenly, Jimmy's voice came from the stage, "Your attention. Please, Scindia and Dominic have made a new decision, there will be no Ring off Ceremony. Scindia doesn't want that, and so Dominic agrees. Without this ceremony, they will be separated. Scindia has accepted the ring as a sign, and Dominic has given his permission, good for them." The whole hall resounded with Applause.

We will go to the dance floor saying one thing, you all know what it is, yet it is a ritual for someone to ask, and today we give this honor to Uncle Joginder Singh. There was Applause. Joginder Singh prepared himself, it was a small thing, but still, he was worried. He also wanted to say two words politely.

"Come on, dad, I know you're the best," said Preet.

Joginder Singh did not know how to say it; he had never been to such a divorce party before and there was no time to ask the children; he had to do something himself.

He got up and said, "Today is a happy day for us, every particle is, in place, don't know what to say to express but I want to dance, give me a good reason." The whole hall applauded.

From the stage, Dominic and Scindia sang together, "Let's dance for freedom." It was too late for him to say anything, the music was loud, and everyone came to the dance floor. Joginder Singh grabbed Mohinder's hand, and she too went on the dance floor. Everyone started dancing to the solo song "Love You Love You, Baby." Mohinder said, "This song is perfect. I have heard it many times. How old is it?"

"This song is almost five decades old, many things have changed, but this song will never change."

"Let's talk about it today." "How nice it is to dance with you all today." "Yes"

"You get lost in the dance when you see my eyes."

"Yes, Jazzy," rolling her eyes at Joginder Singh.

Have I controlled you all my life?"

"No, Jazzy, I love you as you are."

POISON AND NECTAR

T HE SEMINAR WAS over, but many questions were running through Ravi's mind. Among them was a woman who could never be pushed to the margins. There are two reasons for this, Ravi thought while starting the car. The first reason is that even though her idea seemed utterly different from the subject, she expanded its circle instead of dismissing the subject.

Economic reasons for social relationships.

Marriage institution and live-in partner is the main issue. When Ravi received the email, he found the subject very strange and exciting. He registered. On the way back, he was asked if he would like to say something or just be a listener. Ravi preferred to be a listener.

The most important thing that Ravi felt was the age group of participants. Another exciting aspect was that the live-in relationship was dominant. There was tiny talk about the institution of marriage. One could easily have guessed that this ratio could increase further in the future.

Ravi was associated with the institution of marriage and was totally against the live-in relationship. He used to walk around the seminar to understand the economic reasons. Still, Nothing happened, which could mold his static thinking. He returned with a completely different interest. That was the woman with a pretty face who looks like Indian.

Ravi called her in the middle of the break, "Yes, my name is Ravi; it looks like you are Indian."

Asked in English, she replied in Punjabi, "Yes, I am from Punjab, and my name is Simmi."

"How does this session look like?" Ravi said.

"It didn't feel good, and I didn't come here for the session."

Ravi did not consider it appropriate to ask further and thought it would be hasty. Soon the session resumed. The era of different speakers started again. A new topic was not emerging; it seemed that food was being supplied. The same worn-out questions and answers were being repeated. Instead of the effects, the talk was about marriage institution vs. live-in. The marriage institution was considered a waste of time. Ravi was losing interest. He wanted to go; just for Simmi's sake, he did not go.

She sat for the whole session, and Ravi sat for her. After the end of the session, he rushed to Simmi as he already knew; although the hurry was not civilized, Simmi did not feel bad about it.

After a formal conversation, Simmi finds out that he lives alone and is looking for a partner.

Simmi is also looking for a roommate who can share her expenses. Could pay half the rent.

Simmi said, "This is the main reason I came here to find a person who could share my expenses."

It was very appropriate for Ravi when he was separated from his wife; he was looking for a cheap accommodation for the time being. Ravi is optimistic that one day he could reunite with his wife and his child.

Nowadays, he lives in the basement of a room in a townhouse.

His livelihood is like a head covering. Ravi hurriedly introduced himself, and Simmi invited him to her apartment so that they could sit down and talk. After scheduling the evening, Ravi got out and started the car.

During the evening conversation, Ravi realized that Simmi's real name is Simrat, and she has been living in Canada for the last five years. Terms set. Simmi offered to give him a small room out of two bedrooms. Both can make their food in the kitchen. A washroom containing Simmi's products and Ravi can't keep his works there even though the distribution is not proportional. Still, the rent and other expenses of electricity, internet, TV are half. No one will interfere in anyone's life. If anyone wants privacy in the apartment, let another know two days in advance. Simmi will also be the first to watch the TV channel. Ravi can be released at any time, but he will pay the full part of the month. At Simmi's request, he handed over a check for two thousand dollars in advance. One thousand in advance was for rent and one thousand as a damage deposit.

After all the settings were done, Ravi and Simmi started living together. They would go to their work, go back and forth in the evening, eat their food, watch TV and sometimes even talk on some current subject.

Ravi didn't want to go any further, and Simmi was not creating an opportunity.

Simmi was very stone-hearted, rude, and unfriendly.

So rude that Ravi thinks no one can dare to say anything to her. Whenever he tried to talk personally, Simmi would either ignore him or repeat the terms strictly. Whenever she repeated the conditions, Ravi thought that she was considering him an ordinary man. Still, the truth was that Ravi did not want to get into any trouble.

The organization he was associated with and his theoretical motives are profound, but to remain under the influence of others is like engaging in immorality. He sometimes thinks that even if it becomes public that he is living with a woman, the people who know him may get angry.

From college days, he was a comrade of ideas. Now, even though he is no longer proud to be a comrade, he has risen above these things and is bowing his head to his way of life.

How much water had passed under the bridges. The meaning of faith had become negative Among the people now.

Just as a frozen product can be softened over time if it is taken out of the fridge, so can time.

She now began to tolerate Ravi. Whenever Ravi would bring his son for visiting hours, Simmi would fall in love with the kid and go to get some food for him. In this way, she would give Ravi and Sunny a chance to walk and talk alone.

The day came when Ravi told Simmi that his separation was money and only money; he could never earn enough money to buy a house and keep the right car. His wife was never impressed by his ideas to make society better. I think she is not wrong. I can't create a balance, and then we have to separate, but I miss her. She is lovely, and I am very addicted to her body. I miss every curve of her high low hills.

Simmi also said that her broken life is money, but it is not because of less money but because of lots of money. Money that you could not imagine. She came to Canada to manage the money, but now she is tired and wants to get out of the circle in which she is trapped.

After hearing this, Ravi became numb. How can it be possible that someone gets bored with a lot of money?

It also doesn't seem even a person to live in a shared apartment with lots of money, not even a car.

His curiosity grew to know this, but it was not an easy task to learn. Simmi did not seem to be seduced by ideals. She seemed to rise above them. It was not possible to talk about romance; it was against his principles anyway. His emotions could not be played with. Ravi thought it was an impossible task for him. It was not a matter of feeling inferior. Ravi was very handsome and free from any relationship.

Ravi thinks that there is no doubt that he loves his Family very much, but he will work only for his mission even if he is left alone. He is also accountable to the organization, which has made him its secretary.

He chose the wait-and-see formula and tried to help Simmi whenever the opportunity arises. Simmi couldn't guess how much money she had, but with the glitter of money, many dreams flashed before Ravi's eyes. He had also realized that Simmi gets annoyed with any evil thing, so Ravi could not understand where the fine line was.

He needs money for the Family and the organization.

This time when Ravi went to pick up his son Sunny from Tim Horton, Jagmeet also got out of the car and said, "Look, Ravi, we are on our way now; you have no right to try to put pressure on me."

"What happened?" Ravi said briefly.

"I have no complaints with the person you are living with; you have your own life but why she called me is beyond my comprehension. Otherwise, I will have to talk to my lawyer."

"I don't know, Jagmeet, she has called you. I can't say anything about it, but I will answer it next week."

When she started walking back, Ravi said, "Please wait a minute."

"Yes"

"You have an appointment with a neurological doctor at three o'clock tomorrow, do you remember?"

"Thanks, I didn't remember it at all." With that, she left, and Ravi fastened his seat belt and drove off."

It was entirely new for Ravi. Simmi never talked to him affectionately, but why did she call Jagmeet and take her phone from whom? What would Jagmeet think about how ugly I am, living with a woman?

If she has thought like this for even a minute, it is my fault. I haven't been able to tell her in ten years that this is not possible for me. But what about worldly thinking?

He knows very well that I have not been able to make much money because I love my purpose more than money. Suddenly a cyclist came forward, and if Sunny had shouted no to him, the car would have collided with the bicycle. He stopped the car with a loud bang, but Ravi's line of thinking broke.

When the car rolled again, this scene made his mind wander. The combination of car and bicycle matched the thinking of himself and the world. Still, the next moment he thought, why am I always intoxicated with myself? Are the rest of the people not good? They may also consider it. Contemplate and dilemma.

Maybe even Jagmeet can't think that I have anything to do with her. Ravi is getting angry. He decided that he would ask Simmi strictly, or else he would leave the place and settle down anywhere else. It never crossed his mind that had broken up with Jagmeet. He always wants to go back. He thought he had to talk to Simmi today; what does she think, herself?

He doesn't even remember Sunny sitting in the passenger seat next to him.

Simmi arrived at precisely six o'clock. The usual time of her arrival, between six and seven o'clock. Today Ravi did not open the door and did not say anything to her. Simmi also went straight to her room and changed, and came to the living room where Ravi was eagerly waiting for her. "Do you remember your terms or are those terms just for me?" He asked nervously.

Simmi hoped so, but she said softly, "Why, what happened?"

"Did you call my ex?"

"Yes, I did."

"Why?"

"I want to, and there are no such conditions," Simmi said.

"Where did you get the phone?"

"From Sonny, Sonny is my friend, and I didn't need your permission to talk to his mom. you don't have a relationship with Jagmeet anymore, so what difference does it make to you?"

Today is the twentieth day of the month, and I'm moving out at the end of the month. I don't want you to interfere in my life."

Move, I can't hold your hand. With that, Simmi turned on the TV. Simmi knew he would like to know, but the talk would be too long, and her purpose would be lost."

Simmi's silence was unbearable, and Ravi's heart was pounding. He said again, "Why don't you tell me what's in your heart?"

Seeing Ravi's smirking face, Simmi laughed and said, "You are free to do this; move from here, and I will make Jagmeet my roommate, and Sunny will be with me too." What can we get from you?"

Simmi spoke sarcastically so that Ravi's anger would subside, and he could listen to her seriously."

"For God's sake, Jagmeet thinks that I told you to call and you. See Simmi; I love Jagmeet and Sunny very much. If you want to reconcile us, I will be happy and take care of my self-esteem. Tell me what to do."

Simmi turned off the TV and said, "Ravi, you are a very good person. I like you very much because you are different from the rest. I want things to go wrong with your wife, you get divorced, and I get married to you."

"Simmi, you can't imagine this; I know, do the right thing if you have to."

"You have never done anything crazy while living with a woman when I consider all men to be the same. Sometimes I worry that you are coming after me, you will knock on my door in the middle of the night, you will come rushing into the washroom. I have seen many men in my life; I have never met like you. So I want to help you. When I called Jagmeet today, she was very rude to me. She also weighs the relationship between a man and a woman on the same scale. I liked it.

If she were broken with you, She would never dry with me."

"Thanks, Simmy; it looks like we've become friends, not just roommates."

Simmi got up and extended her hand towards Ravi and said, "Would you like to be my friend?"

"Of course, I do."

Ravi not only shook hands but got up and took Simmi in his arms.

Simmi's eyes widened. The stoned eyes filled with tears.

I did everything in a hurry, but one thing pops up, I could not see her soft corner for you otherwise.

"Jagmeet is very good, no doubt about it, but she doesn't know how to live life. Looking around, she also wants to compete with the people. It looks like she's about to make a dollar. Who doesn't love making dollars now? My opinion is that if you live a comfortable life, you will gradually be blessed. The ones she wants to compete with, don't think about when they came? By the way, she is fine; I also don't earn many dollars, I didn't get a good job, I don't do two jobs like others. things got worse."

"Don't worry; the solution will come out. I have a completely different cycle than you. I don't have a problem with money, there are millions, but I am not married. Not even getting it done now, my mother died thinking of my marriage."

"How, when?"

"Ravi, this is a very long narration. My mother was not really dead, but her soul was crushed, and how long could the body breathe. The answer was yes, the body was dead too, and she was gone long ago."

"If you want to talk, say calmly, don't be fooled by philosophies," Ravi said.

"Let's get some milk first; I am emotional now; I want to detach from this emotional mood.

Otherwise, these philosophies will come automatically; I have no emphasis on them."

They were walking; they didn't need a car for milk. The weather was fine today anyway. Then Simmi said, "Ravi, how proud are you of yourself?"

"Why…there is no pride? I'm just living comfortably."

"Never wandered?"

"Simmi, I don't understand what you mean."

"There are many meanings, but I ask directly, has there ever been a desire to have a relationship with a woman?" It's widespread in men."

"I don't know, never thought."

"Didn't you think, or did the situation never arise?"

"I never really thought about it."

"Simmi, I am not a person, I belong to an institution.

Vishwamitra but

"If the time comes, when the music starts its tunes, will you turn off the music of desire?"

If the time has come and maybe, I start thinking differently. Perhaps I compare that part with Jagmeet. I "Now you are thinking of milk only, as long as I know. I am going to A. T. M. Now you go and get milk alone. do. Don't overthink about milky-Jagmeet." Simmi said.

Let's go."

Ravi went to the corner store, and Simmi thought in her heart that once Maneka would dance, let's see if he passes or fails.

On return, the bag of milk was in Ravi's hand, and Simmi opened the lock with her key.

"Yes, and you mean that you only listen to the heart, listen to the voice of the Spirit, and have never done anything wrong?"

"Simmi, I make tea first; you have asked the question which has Nothing to do with us. Such thinking cannot be expected from you. It is not you but the world around you that is speaking."

Simmi got up and went to the washroom, and when she came back, she was wearing shorts and a deep low cut top.

The top was not what she used to wear every day. Ravi came into the living room with two cups of tea. He didn't pay any attention to Simmi's outfit and took a sip of tea comfortably. The tea was still scalding.

"Oh... my God."

"Why what happens?" Simmi asked with a smile.

"The hot tea went into my mouth."

"Where is your focus?" Simmi was sure that she must have gotten into a trance because of my attire.

Ravi hadn't even looked at her.

He looked at her and said, "Come on, you have become a model look like a cartoon; I have never seen you in such clothes before."

Simmi agreed in her heart but remained silent. She thought her thoughts were in vain, but no problem; there are still many more arrows. How long will the hen be happy?

"Come on; you probably wanted to say something."

"I don't remember."

"You wanted to say something about your mother or your marriage. It was something like that."

Simmi remembered that she was going to tell her story. She was emotional and had forgotten her true purpose. She began to wonder how she had become so weak for the first time. How did her thoughts about men change, and what should she do now?

"Ravi, I have hidden one thing from you."

"What?"

"I drink when I'm stressed. Will you join me in the drink?"

"No, Simmi, I never have drunk alcohol in my life. You take a drink; if you want to, I don't mind. Many of my friends drink. I never felt bad about sitting with them. You are my friend too, get your drink and drink without hesitation but for God's sake change your clothes too, you don't look `Simmi` in these clothes at all."

Simmi went to her room. She took one shot of whisky, hurriedly changed her clothes, filled glass, and came out.

The first Dram kicked her off her feet. She started strangely looking at Ravi. She sipped and said, "Ask me, what do you want?"

"Simmi, I don't ask anything, we were talking about your mother, and you wanted to say something. I am not personally interested in it, but I would be happy to help and give some moral support."

Simmi had drunk a lot of times but never felt like she was doing today. She thought she was not Simmi, just a woman, and for the first time today, she was sitting with someone who looked like her. Even my cousin's brother did not help me when I need help.

Ravi just smiled and said, "Say as you wish, say no, friend, don't understand, but tell your story and lighten the burden on your heart."

"All right, Ravi, I will tell you the whole story but don't even talk anymore, don't interpret me, don't poke your nose with any of your philosophy. First, listen. I am not what I look like to you. You are also a strange person. We will talk after. If we can't get it, then you have to move. "Simmi said under the influence of alcohol.

Ravi smiled and said, "As you wish, I am just listening."

Simmi sipped and said, "Listen to me carefully. let me tell you one thing first; you were the secretary of the New India Workers association in India."

Ravi was speechless and said, "Oh my God, how do you know?"

"I know a lot. I also know what your relationship with Meena was? How she was made General Secretary? She got engaged, but you promised her to get married. She broke up with her fiancée. We don't know what happens after, but you married Jagmeet and came to Canada."

"What else do you know?"

"My first meeting at the seminar with you is manipulated. I knew two days ago that you were coming. I'll open your email. You don't know when it was hacked. Jagmeet's phone number, which was not given to me by Sunny, is already in our file. There is an agency behind you, and the agency has given me your file. Everything is happening according to us. It will continue to happen, according to us."

"I am surprised, but there is no fear. It's also good to have the opportunity to learn about a poisonous girl. But that is okay. Tell me about your mother. This word is common for us to talk.

Ravi said, and Simmi did not respond and said, "Now listen to my story."

Ravi turned his side on the sofa and said, "Yes, I will listen carefully. but let me tell you that everything else is nonsense about Meena; that's why he left the country." Believe it or not, I have become accustomed to accusations. It was Meena's decision, not mine.

Simmi closed her eyes as if choosing words or going back in time, and then she said, "We studied together till the fifth class. He did not know that I like him when he left. The little girl knows what love is. It seemed to me that something was empty in the sixth grade, but I never understood why it was empty.

My hell story begins when he returns twelve years later. I was young. His uncle lived in our neighborhood. His scent wafted through the clay wall into our yard. I was overwhelmed by the fragrance. I don't know if he was aware of that or not, but I was as happy as if the whole world under my feet.

Passing by, we look at each other and wait to see each other again, and that is what is called love, but it was not a love affair, it was a flashback, a flashback of a girl. He was handsome, I now understand that he caught me. It was beautiful and plentiful, but I did not see its truth hidden behind the shape for a long time. That's why I hate every man, Ravi too."

Ravi laughed and said, "Leave me alone. I'm not a man in this story; I'm just a friend."

"His broad chest was enough to hold me close. I was a beautiful girl too. Please don't go to my present situation, now every limb Withers but at some point, the boys used to slow down when they saw me. I used to think that it was not the boys' fault. My limbs were like that. I was trembling at every step while walking. One of the things I liked about him was that he cared a lot about his health, but it turned out to be my delusion. Our discussion started around the village. We became physical quickly.

One day I met a lovely girl. She told me a few things about him. "He is a pimp of political leaders and supplies them, call girls. I did not believe and asked him. He explains, and I think of him.

Now you will be in a hurry to ask his name but leave out the title. Violence and brutality have no name. Even the beauty that melts has no name. We are both anonymous; one of the reasons is that we are the story's characters, and this story is similar to every girl. He also had an old car, which I never knew where he got it from because neither he was earning anything, nor his father was able to give it to him. Suffice it to say that the car was the car he loved me; the way he loved me was different, playing with limbs, twisting them, never talking to the heart, just me and his habits. Well, now I wonder how any girl could have gone as far as I was. He even pulled my hair in anger. You tell me where to go with a bunch of hair when the people around are afraid of him.

One thought of mine that it would get better, or I would improve it, but the turn came to the point that I found it difficult to defend myself.

The shape was not so pale yet. We were fragrant, but no boy would even look at me.

It seemed like I was just like his mistress. Marriage bond.

He did not like the name of marriage, but my mother's dream was to get married. Now, who can explain to my mother what I have left for the wedding? Whenever he danced at me, I forgot myself and did everything he used to, just to please him. Later I would be relieved to see him satisfied.

Sometimes the situation would get better, but I didn't know why it got better. I found out I was pregnant. The day I told him he was drunk. Even that night, his behavior did not change.

My intensity came under suspicion. When crazy woke up in the morning, the idiot suggested an easy solution, get an abortion.

His words were the words of a stone on which not a drop of love could stay. That evening I told him he had to decide. He wants Family or your own imperfect life. I didn't know anything about his evil deeds; now, I was convinced that he must have done something wrong. Might be smugglers or gangsters. The question of my decision made him angry, and he did to me what you can't even imagine. You would have thought that someone would have punched you, but no, I was used to punching. I had already surrendered to his violence, I just needed a roof so that my widowed mother would not die with guilt. He did that night what I was ashamed to do when I was pregnant.

When things got worse, I had an abortion to save my mother. My body was squeezed that day, I was crying, and he was laughing with someone in the cell. Don't think, Ravi, that I am a lame person.

No, it was not a matter of being a poor girl; it was a matter of grief for the mother who wanted to be safe in society by putting her hand on her son-in-law's head by all means. Suppose I don't feel worried about my mother. I did not tell my mother anything and continued to tolerate abuse. His car was old, but there was no shortage of money; his pockets were always full. I am convinced that he must be doing something illegal. The state of happiness was fixed on him, but I had lost consciousness.

I thought to tell my mother that we got married in court or ask him to get married only to please my mother.

Later, even if you want to keep me as it is, you could marry someone else. I am ready for that.

In those days, my cousin was transferred to our city, he was an inspector in the police, and according to him, he was going to become a DSP very soon. My cousin came to our town to join the report. I stayed with us. After the formal meeting, my mother told him the whole story.

He promised that he would get them married, aunt, don't worry, it is my duty now.

The mother was relieved, and on the fourth day, she died.

My cousin made all the preparations for the funeral, and the relatives would come and go with regret. I was now alone in the world, and I trusted my cousin only.

My way of life became such that sometimes I would spend time in a house in this city and sometimes in a hotel in another town. There was no point in asking what was going on because he would have a contrived answer as to why you are worried, I will build a house somewhere. These were the days when I decided to take revenge on him. My heart admitted that he was my mother's killer.

One day my cousin's door opened too. He had come to our house. When he asked his name, and I told him his name was Darshan, the cousin was surprised and said, "Look, Simmi, I can talk to him, but I can't force him without his consent."

"DSP cousin started walking around, and I found out that he is also afraid of Darshan. Sometimes I wonder if he would have done the same if I had been his real sister? Maybe that's how it is; the world is no longer what my mother saw it to be. The healed mother died."

Then one day two men came to visit us in a city hotel. At first glance, they seemed political. The three of them drank together, and I sat in a corner, they kept ordering, and I provided what they need.

After they left, he fell in love with me, as if he had found something. The next day we went to the bank and opened a joined account and one sole store in my name 'and deposited Rs. 50,000 in it, it was a matter of great happiness for me. That evening, we went to the house of a woman, Purnima, the Mahila Women Liberation Struggle Committee chairperson.

She filled out the form and made me the member. Everything was going without my consent. I could not understand. Still, I am happy.

My head, but still, it was a good omen. We would have stayed there for two hours, and during that time, there would have been about thirty phone calls every five minutes. The living room of the woman's house was also excellent. In the art paintings, the woman's nakedness was beating. It is the turning point for me. He thought he is using me, but now I decided that I would poison his life from this point.

Gradually he started associating me with the big society. I was introduced as a social worker.

, all the city women believed in him.

The lie was not understood, while the truth was that I was not a social worker. I hardly know the person living next door.

Back in our hometown, we both made our own will to nominate each other as our beneficiaries.

My satisfaction was growing. I felt safe now. The seed that was sown in me was only being nurtured now, but it did not last long.

Darshan never loved me; I know maybe he didn't even love himself. Everything was going on like a team and one day got a call from my cousin, he had something to do with Darshan, and he was asking me to recommend him."

That night Darshan was not mine. Now my snakes were looking for Darshan. When and how my poison starts working.

I learned the same black knowledge that he knew and used on everyone, even on his girl.

"You are a very dangerous woman," Ravi told her to deepen his words.

"Yes, Ravi, but you don't have to be afraid. The serpent only bites the one who is afraid. Why should you be afraid of, so don't worry."

"Just kidding, I am listening about your cousin."

"Nothing about my cousin is worth listening. Thanks to my mother, I got her work done from Darshan without any hesitation, but it broke a lot inside me. It seemed that even my cousin thought I was a prostitute. Now I knew I was the only one in the world, and I was determined to be strong."

"I decided to have a deeper relationship with Purnima, but that decision was not mine but the networks. If someone else had taken my place, she would have made the same decision in such a situation. Surprisingly for me, Purnima knew I would come to her.

"As soon as I met Purnima, she took me to the executive of her women's wing, the Close Circle. Sometimes it happens that you don't even know the next one well, and she sits on your head. But this is not Simmi, but Simmi's amazing beautiful woman's curved body."

"I did not tell this to Darshan, and when he found out, he fought with me a lot. My heart said this is now the back count of Darshan. Maybe once or twice more, this fight and then this fight will end."

"It was the annual meeting of the Women's Liberation Struggle Committee. I also went with Purnima. I had to take stock of the whole year, and in the same session, I was made the cashier at the suggestion of Purnima. I was shocked to see the account and could never have imagined that there would be such a large amount. The next day, the meeting's report came in the newspapers, and according to that news, I had become a star from a social worker. It was not all because of Purnima but to push me even more profoundly.

I took the newspaper and went to Purnima's house to thank her. She was alone today and told her manager not to let anyone in or answer any phone.

That's when Ravi's cell phone rang. Sunny was on the other side. Ravi went to the balcony for about five minutes, and Simmi turned up the TV volume.

Ravi came back and said curiously, "Then what happened? I feel like watching a movie."

"Yes, Ravi, this is a movie to listen to but not a movie for the characters."

"Purnima looks very smart, and so does your boss."

"No, Ravi, she is also the part of the system but a lot more significant than me.

"The next thing she did was turn on the TV and play a DVD. After a Hindi song, there was a movie of me and Darshan in which we were in bed naked and doing."

"I was not bothered, and Purnima said it is necessary, nothing to worry about, it is just a guarantee, you have to handle that much money."

"Is it Darshan behind this?"

Darshan doesn't even know; he doesn't see and doesn't need it. He trusted everything with his eyes closed. There are so many cases against him that he can't handle it."

"What do you want from me, Purnima?" I asked.

"Congratulations, you're going to Canada. This decision is not mine but the executives.

"Will Darshan be with me?"

"Why, aren't you satisfied with him yet?" Purnima said with a laugh.

"If I can, I'll shoot him. I just asked, 'It's better if he's not with me.'

"Is Canada going to be permanent or a visitor?"

"No, not sure. Don't even try to be sure. Who knows if you will be called back for some other important work?" We are not getting smart people for Europe."

I said to Purnima, "By the way, I am not capable of making conditions. May I make a request?"

"What can I do for you?"

"Purnima Ji, please make Darshan a big zero. I just hate him."

"Simmi, it would be done.

He made him zero.

Everybody is fed up with him. You are not alone.

His screws would be tightened before you go to Canada. I can make this promise to you."

"How long have you been in Canada?" Ravi asked.

"Fifth years now, I have multiple visas, sometimes here and there."

"What do you do for a living?"

"Ravi, it is out of your jurisdiction to ask this. I have your file; I want to warn you about it."

"What kind of file, I've never done anything wrong?"

"No one will ask you what's wrong. What exactly is it? That too is beyond your power."

"Then tell me one thing?"

"Ask?"

"Are you a human or an alien?"

"Ravi, this question can only be asked by someone who hopes for a change. Do you hope so?"

"No."

"Then, just think about how to breathe in what is happening."

"Then what I think, how to sleep with the beautiful girl who is sitting in front of me?"

"It's okay to think about it, but also think about my world. Will you bear my sting? The lotus does not beat. Even though we are snakes, we still live on Earth.

"Just be careful not to talk about changing the system. You are not a teenager now.

Someone here has reported that you are setting up an organization in Canada against your homeland, Jagmeet, may have said."

"No, Simmi, Jagmeet can't even think."

"I know on my own; you are not involved in any work, maybe the articles you have written are coming in your way. But anyway, don't worry, I have never seen a person like you before. When I see you, I miss my mother."

Ravi now was under stress, not understand what was happening, what Simmi was saying. Seeing him silently, Simmi laughed and said, "Oh, how good it would be if my mother looked at you, and you would be my husband today."

"Looks like your intention is not right, don't you think negative. You cannot rape me. I am stronger than you." Ravi said with a smile.

"Okay, do you want a try? "Simmi also smiled back.

"Let's talk seriously; I want you and Jagmeet to be reconciled and Sunny to be with you both and become a better person. I love sonny. What can I do about it?"

"First, we have to check what your ability is. Will you be able to reach Sunny? And Jagmeet would trust your reach for Sonny. She is the only one to decide. She is the mother of the Family?" I know you are a great person, but Jagmeet...You better work on Jagmeet." Ravi suggested the right path.

"Okay, you have concluded, but you should also remember that when poison turns to nectar, what it could do."

"Let me tell you one thing, Simmi, that I believe in you, and those who believe do not care about poison or nectar."

"Ravi, relationships have no name; Sunny's responsibility is mine too, "Simmi sighed and said, even though I will have no existence in your life, it is a fragrance that will keep me alive for the rest of life." You do not know that the scorched souls may be black, but the effect is not black."

"You don't need a pot of words; you can unite our Family; I know you have power. I believe your nectar. there is so much power in you."

"Strength belongs to my mother; she will do everything. she never dies, always living in me."

"Yes, Simmi, mother never dies. Yes, the elixirs of her faith, for a short time, become poison, but they do not die doing the elixir."

"Ravi elixirs have only strength, not emotion."

Tears started flowing from Ravi's eyes.

Simmi quietly went to the kitchen. He embraces the bottle in her mouth instead of the peg. Nectar did not know how much poison she drank and came out and started crying. Her condition was like crazy. Ravi got up and tried to console her.

He took her in his arms.

She became even more glued to him. Ravi touched her head. Simmi unleashed her fingers open in Ravi's hair.

Drizzlingly joined the limbs. They were left behind, shivering, somewhere on the body.

Gluing together in one Samadhi

The union of souls was going to embrace. Bodies were not there. No traditions, no values.

The body could be touched, could be possessive, could be married but not the soul.

Earth is circled. Sun is blessing the Earth.

Once upon a time, Ravi's traditional clothes were being taken off. The world was getting naked. Nectar was being revealed.

Traditions were creating a new definition. Poison and nectar were armpits

The world, changing many colors,

The weeds were shaking with the wind.

Lots of flowers somewhere in the world. Eve and Adam had forgotten everything beyond their tasted fruit.

THE LOST NECKLACE

AVE YOU EVER been to the villages of Ontario? Have you met the people there?

I have met many times. Every time I think about how good people are, just like my own ancestors who lived close to nature. Much has changed in the last ten years. New projects are coming. Houses are being built, but it doesn't look like their hearts will change. Horse stables will remain the same. The horse-carts will keep moving. The children sitting in them will keep waving goodbye to every passing car. It is the effect of humanity. They will keep thinking about taking care of the environment.

Their eagerness to show the way to the lost people would be the same.

Curiosity to know more about them will remain intact.

Now it comes to a woman living in a village.

I found a shipping office in Chatham.

I found that office in Google search.

It's been six years since I left the truck job.

And I had the same effect on my mind about the village of Ontario.

I called the shipping office, and Laila responds to my call. I explained the whole problem that I want to bring some product from India by ship.

Nothing to worry about, just let me know the details; we are here to help you.

"Where do you live?"

"Brampton," I answered.

"You have to come to our office at Chatham once. We don't have an office in Toronto or nearby. You know a small company with a big heart. We talk, if you are interested, you have to sign some papers. We are the best in this business for small shipping as you told me. After you could check our rates with any other company."

"Why are your rates so nominal?"

"Because our overhead expenses are much less compared to others. So you are in good hands, don't worry."

I was impressed. I want to see Laila. Though the name is lovely, it also has a friendly attitude; let's see Laila and shipping.

The next day I went to Chatham. The name Laila is widespread in India. Laila is a historical character, the Girlfriend of Majnu, who died for each other

It seemed like she was having a lot of fun in her childhood.

The mouth was as if bathed in milk. Body parts as if they were placed in a showroom. The nose was long, and the chin was like a match of the nose slightly more extended and more in-depth in the middle. Wide eyes, uncensored eyebrows were saying that there was no need for a significant cut, forehead hair as if lying in the path of a rebellion. The ears were the same as all the women, but the earrings Smirking look at me too.

The green top was matching with earrings. Stretch genes are common to all, but Laila's genes were the most eye-catching.

I was not seeing her as an office-bearer but looking at her as a beautiful girl.

Laila later said when I asked her that she was not surprised, it is normal for her, and she is relatively happy, and if someone says something on the spot, she will thank him. I said, "Laila, we don't compliment anyone without meaning; it's uncivilized."

"Yes, we all have our criteria for being uncivilized, but I have always wanted to know the criteria for different people."

"Mr. Chandan, you are in good hands now. I understand your point. You do not need to take the whole container. Our job is to complete the container, and we will charge according to the weight and volume of your goods in proportion to the entire container. Yes, the only problem is that sometimes there is a slight delay. We do not load the ship until the container booked in our ship is completed; that is why there may be a slight delay. Still, this delay is not more than three weeks at most, and it is a good idea that your goods have no expiry date, just clothes. Good deal for you."

"Thanks, Laila, good for you too to have my job.

"Of course, Chandan, this is business; save money together. In business, every penny counts." I was happy too because the most significant concern was shipping; on this occasion, everything that Laila said was very tempting for me. Our conversation lasted for about an hour, and it was decided to take the goods from my shipper and deliver the goods to my house, exempting them from Canadian customs duty. Laila also demanded $800 from me. I signed a machine copy of the credit card on the condition that the amount would remain on hold. The number I mentioned was approximate. The growth deficit was to come later. I shook hands with Laila and walked back.

When I came out, it was raining. I suddenly remembered that I had to call my wife. Thankfully, it came to mind just in time. It was a two and a half-hour drive. I had to come one time to sign the contract; then all the work had to be done by email or phone.

The next day Laila's phone rang, saying Mr. Chandan could save you some more money if you asked your shipper to talk to a trucking company to deliver the goods to Mumbai. In India, those with whom our company deals charge more." "Yes, why not Laila?" Every penny counts."

"And you remember me, Mr. Chandan?"

"Yes, I remember everything about beautiful girls."

"Thanks, Mr. Chandan, you called me beautiful, but I'm not a girl, now my daughter is a girl, she studies at the University of Toronto at Toronto. I am a woman, and now I am on my way to becoming an old woman."

"No, Laila, you are so beautiful and so maintained that you can be compared to any lake, rising sun redness, rays, whatever."

Laila laughed at my words and said, "What is 'Whatever,' Mr. Chandan?"

"Men call it Tir Tukka. Yes, we men all understand; women like this kind of poetic nonsense. Just seize the opportunity."

"What is the meaning of Tir Tukka in English."

"I don't know exactly, but we could say blind arrow."

"Oh, just like a blind date?"

"Of course, Laila, now you got my point."

"By the way, Mr. Chandan, apart from business, what is your hobby?"

"Laila, I am a social activist and currently working on domestic violence."

"Great, I'm glad to meet you, Mr. Chandan; accept the standing ovation."

"Let's ask your shipper and tell him how much it will cost if he arranges; if it is less, then we will ship to Mumbai through him. If there is a slight difference, then we will follow the quotation. Good Mr. Chandan, good night."

"I will try, or you talk yourself with my shipper I will email you his phone number."

"That's great, send me his phone number. I will call, see what he said."

"All right, honey, I will call you tomorrow."

She hangs up the phone.

"Whose phone was it?" A voice came from the kitchen.

"It belonged to a shipping company."

I laid down on the sofa and closed my eyes. Now I imagine in my brain thoughts.

Laila got up from her seat. I delusion she seemed to stand up to me and speak truthfully.

I was even more amazed and said, "My work on domestic violence is widespread.

The topics have grown so much that it is now becoming a thesis."

Laila looked deep into my eyes. I realized that it seems to be stuck now. Truth be told, gossips are high in society around.

Laila was impressed.

"Hello ... why are you, numb?" Haven't you ever seen a social activist?"

"I wonder what a strange coincidence it is, the work I am doing is the same, but my work is not a volunteer work like yours. Rather, it adds to my meaning. I wish I could serve society like you, as a hobby. What other hobbies do you have?"

"Yes, the second hobby is trapping women."

Laila giggled and laughed, "You naughty boy, you're interesting, you can be friends with."

"Why not, but we don't have a tradition of befriending women."

"Why is that?"

"I don't know, I like it, but we don't like it."

"I mean in your research, during the study of domestic violence, has there ever been a reason for this?"

"Yes, this is the root of the great reason for domestic violence."

"It simply came to our notice then. But why ..., well, there will be some of your tradition, but what is the harm in it? If you can befriend a man, why not a woman? Doesn't your wife have any male friends?"

"No, please, God."

"Don't you want to live as you please? It is to please the partner, not to punish, there will be a tradition." Laila connects everything with tradition.

"Good night, honey," I said and hung up.

"Why are you muttering.?"

"What, I was just sleeping."

"You say something while sleeping; I think you are calling me."

"Would you like a consultation?"

"Talk to you in the morning; I know what you're talking about."

"No, that's not the point; it's something else."

Anyway, at least I didn't go down without explaining myself first. I don't hear the daily squeals. I have to check my email first, then read the online newspaper and then go to Walk, come back, and it will be ten o'clock, so I don't have time Today, we will talk tomorrow.

There was silence in the kitchen.

When I woke up in the morning and had a headache, I made tea and drank it. Before I woke up, my wife had gone to work, so I feel relaxed. Gradually the two girls woke up; the boy was still asleep. Wakes up at four o'clock in the evening, stays up all night on the computer. The commotion in the house was like a railway platform. Different voices, hot tea, hot snacks, requests were being made to the passengers. Do not touch any unattended items; take care of your things.

I did the rest myself in the kitchen. I don't know if there is a bomb in the luggage. It bursts as soon as you touch it. I am the only un-attended item in this house, and this emptiness is for me. Everyone is taking care of it, don't know when this bomb will explode, and the journey will be incomplete. It seemed like no one cared. All the coincidences are together on one platform and waiting for their train.

I had just taken a shower when the phone rang. My heartbeat said it must have belonged to Laila, but it belonged to a duct cleaner. Today was Friday, and on this day, My wife, Madam Sunil, would arrive an hour earlier. It, too, was a difficult task. I was sipping tea at about eleven o'clock when Laila's phone rang.

"Hi, Mr. Chandan, how are you?" Did you find out from your shipper?"

"No, not yet. I'll call India tonight and tell you tomorrow."

"Mr. Chandan, I'm coming to Toronto tomorrow, to my daughter. I will arrive at ten o'clock. The time to meet her is at eleven o'clock, I will stay with her for two hours and leave at one o'clock in the afternoon. The rest of the day I have to spend in Toronto. My hubby is not coming with me. Can you give me company?"

"Of course, tell me where to come; I'll come and discuss everything that shipper from India would tell me."

"Super ... let's meet again tomorrow."

Even at this age, if there is any excitement, it was happening to me. Sunil also came at the right time; I also liked her Today."

"Are you looking so happy today?"

"Looks like my train was on time."

"I don't understand; I'm always on time, but why so happy today?"

"Dude, today is Friday, don't you remember?"

"Oh yeah, let's make your favorite Chinese food today."

"Leave the food, sit with me for a while."

"No fun like before, remember what we used to do on Friday, now we are old, now the children are young, now we are worried about them. I was supposed to talk to you yesterday, but seeing your mood, I kept quiet."

"What is this?"

"Yes, little Bunty is upset. She says I can't befriend an Indian boy. It seemed like she didn't like the Indians at all, but now that it is known that she has a friendship with an Italian, she stayed with him last Friday night; I lied to you that she went to her friend's Henna".

"Oh my God, what are you saying?"

"Yes, I can't sleep at night; I kept the veil from you. I thought you would be upset, I would handle myself, but now it's over, so I have to tell you. Bunty told me that if we force her for anything, she will leave the house."

I thought for a while and said, "I don't think it's time to force her anymore, don't say anything yet; let's take a break." Later on, say good things about the richness of our traditions. These colorful people form relationships just to have fun, and after a few years later, who are you and who am I."

"Yeah, Al, that sounds pretty crap to me; looks like, in this world, nobody cares for me. I am alone in this world, not even you. I am in a deep depression. Everyone is playing with their duffel."

"You are so heartbroken. Let me handle this. Please don't say anything right now; don't talk about any relationship. Just talk about your culture. After all, Bunty is your daughter. She will listen if you listen to her properly."

"Yes, you are right. Just tell me more; time is slipping."

"Sunil, take an Indian calendar and watch every festival, fasts, and any crap, which belongs to our family. Celebrate all those days. Let's see the result."

"All right, Chandan."

On Saturday afternoon, the clock slowed down even more, as if it had run out of gas. It was not immediately clear if Laila had arrived in Toronto. I was annoyed; at least, Laila should inform me of her arrival in Toronto.

I was thinking about Bunty, how cherished she is, caress her more than other kids. Now she will make our old age cry.

The phone rang, breaks my chain of thought. In response to my hello, Laila continued, "Hi, handsome, good morning."

"Good morning," I looked at Sunil before saying anything further. Sunil was watching a serial on TV. "OK, I'll get there, OK." I hung up the phone in the usual manner.

"Whose phone was it?" Sunil asked.

"Why do you check-up all the time? The girl's attention is not taken care of by you, which is your responsibility. You keep asking for an account of my phones all the time.

There was an insurance person. I have started getting third party auto insurance. Our insurance company has gone to extremes."

Sunil did not pay much attention to my talk. She was watching TV serial keenly.

"There was a lot of fuss in the serial as well. A necklace was missing from the house. Sunil was also probably guessing about the chain; I don't know why these women have to guess-disease? 'I got up and grabbed the car key and went out. Coming in the car, I breathed a sigh of relief and got the car through the university.

Laila was supposed to be free at three o'clock after meet her daughter. I arrived at two-thirty. Laila was to come to the Bay Street 'star Cup coffee shop' on Bay Street. I took two or three rounds and sat down in the coffee shop corner at quarter to three. My hypothesis started talking. I was thinking a lot upside down, but one thing was for sure, don't rush. First, you have to read Laila's mind; where can I find a woman like Laila at this age? There is no room for any mistake. I should be cautious.

The last five minutes after three o'clock were tough when Laila arrived. "Hi, handsome," Laila called me. I pretended not to see her. I saw her when she turns.

"Hey Laila, how are you, have a seat."

Laila sat down on the chair and said, "I need something to eat; I'm starving. Will you eat something too?"

"No, I had lunch late; I'll just have coffee, medium single sugar, double cream."

"All right," Laila walked over to the counter. I thought I should have gone, but too late now.

Laila was still sitting when her cell spoke.

"Hi Michael, yes, I have arrived."

"No, no, I won't go for a walk in the evening, you know, my driving, I'll stay the night here, in a motel." I will leave at seven o'clock in the morning and reach you at ten o'clock."

She looks like slut, I thought. I don't know exactly where she will spend the night. Who is Michael, where she will go in the morning? If it will be tonight and this Michael must be a friend too. These people just have fun. Our way of life is terrible. Stick to the shackles and vomit all your life; she lives in the village, not even the town.

OK, Bye, Laila was about to hang up when I came out of my thoughts.

"Yes, what is the program, handsome?" Laila asked me a question.

"As government orders."

"You tell Chandan how much time do you have? I am idle the remaining day and tonight. Michael called me, telling him I'd be back in the morning."

"Who is Michael?" I nodded and asked.

"My husband." Laila's answered.

"Where will you stay at night?"

"In the motel, my husband's brother lives here, but I don't have a tuning in with him, and Michael knows, so whenever I come to Toronto, I stay in the motel and drink a lot at night." And I snore and rest all night. Where do you find time in your home to do this? Michael would laugh and say, pick up Mickey, go to a bar and hit two pegs; you have to drive in the morning or walk in the afternoon. You know, he's so funny."

"I find it very strange, Laila, that you live in a motel like this. We don't do that. My wife and I can never spend the night alone in a motel."

"Is she scared?" Laila asked in surprise.

"Not afraid, not at all."

"If she's scared, she can do it in someone's company, friends, or somebody acquainted."

"No, it's not like that; it's not our tradition."

"What kind of tradition is it for women to sleep or stay in a motel or something like that?" Laila asked in surprise.

"I don't know; it's just not a tradition."

"It's not like the name of the tradition, but you don't trust your wife?"

"No, it's not like that, but ... I don't know ... it doesn't happen to us."

"It's interesting to talk to you." Laila looked me straight in the eye. Our coffee and Laila had finished eating. We got up and walked out without being asked.

"Where are we going now?" Laila asked as if everything depended on me.

"Where do you want to go?" I asked.

"It depends on how much time you have. First, I want to see the movie 'Captain Philip.' Then I will go around Eaton Center; then I will enjoy the lights of downtown at night. Then I will go to sleep in the motel, now tell me, where will you leave me in all this?"

"I don't know." I expressed my confusion.

"That's right; I called your shipper. At first, he had a problem with English, then he called someone and brought him on the phone. The rates they are offering are lower than our rates. Do this; trust me. In this case, I will save some of your dollars. OK, handsome?"

My focus was not on rates; I wondered how to ask her if I could spend the night with her.

"By the way, Laila, I am idle till evening, but I have to go home for an hour at eight o'clock in the evening. If you say so, I can rejoin you after nine o'clock."

"That's Great! I'm excited to spend time with you."

I turned around and said, "Yes, Laila, you do the shipping. I trust you."

"O.K. then, Leave it on me now."

After watching the movie, I went home with permission. I promised that I would reach the motel at precisely ten o'clock and then discuss the issues.

There was chaos in my mind. Sunil was sitting at home shaking her fortune, and Bunty was out of the house again Today. Today she made no excuses and told Mom that it was a friend's birthday, and after that, she would stay with Dominic and come in the morning. Saying this, she was only informing Mom, not asking for her permission. That was why Sunil was very sad Today. He needed my help, but I was in a hurry to go to Laila.

On the way, I also bought a packet for safety from the convenience store.

Laila opened the door when I knocked at the motel; she talked to someone on the phone.

She saw me and hung up the phone, or the talk was over, I could not get any result. What is all this? Why did Laila call me at night in the motel room? The questions were waiting to be answered. It was not a happy occasion for me. Don't know what I was thinking? Sunil's sadness, Bunty being out of the house at this time, or Laila being in the same room with me, these three hammers were knocking on my head.

"Hello handsome, what are you thinking?" Laila broke my chain of thoughts.

"I was thinking about you, Laila. How happy you are. I wish my wife were like you."

"Isn't she like your wife?"

"No.,"

"Tell me why what's the problem, we'll find a solution. I'll be happy to help you." It is also my subject."

"What is your subject?"

I did my M.A. in Sociology, and now the research is underway."

"On what topic?" I asked.

"Gender complexes in different nations."

"Oh, Great!"

A lot of work has been done. I have also done a lot of surveys about your Punjabi culture. According to surveys, there have been some bizarre revelations."

"What kind of revelations? I asked in surprise and curiosity.

"Sit down first, and then we talk. Before you came, I was talking to Michael, my husband. I told him that you were coming and that you would stay the night with me. He said hi to you."

"Thank you, Michael." Laila laughed and said, "Where is Michael here, handsome?"

"Sitting in your heart, looking at me, where else?" I was so confused that even Laila didn't think anything wrong about me. The rest was up to Laila. There was nothing that I did to cause. Then what was the harm in making numbers?

Laila sipped the peg and said, "Handsome, I don't want to hide from you. Can I record our conversation? I need your permission as required by law. Before you permit me, I have to tell you that confidentiality must be maintained. Your name would not be mentioned without your express permission. I will acknowledge you in my thesis if you want to.

After all, nowadays, they do not accept these without documents.

"Sure, whatever you do, you are free from my side.

If you want, you can do whatever comes to your mind in this romantic time."

"You naughty boy, don't worry, I have no intention of raping you."

"Isn't it in the mood to rape today?"

"No, we don't believe in rape. We just believe in love."

"Haven't you fallen in love yet?"

"Let's stop the mischief and sit down well. If you want to have some hot shots, get it yourself. I don't know what you like. Everything is on the table, whiskey, scotch, vodka. Rye. I have whiskey. I have taken one; I will take another and two before going to bed."

Laila took out the recorder and placed it on the table.

"Before you start talking, tell me one thing, what are your thoughts on this topic as a typical Punjabi?"

"But what is the question? Tell me straight."

"The question is, how do you feel when you meet a woman? Don't feel any guilt. Many nations are embroiled in this question. Not only men but also women do not take this question lightly."

"What can I say? I don't understand."

"Let me make it even easier for you. How do you think about me? Do you think that you can mold me to your liking? And tell me, do you feel any gender complex when you talk to me?"

"Yes, I feel. I feel that you are a woman; you are beautiful; I wish I could take you and go to bed. But I will not do that. Are you happy now?"

"You will not do this because your heart does not believe, but the mind says there is no harm. Is that OK?"

"No, that's not right. I don't know. The heart is not the mind. No sound has come from within yet, neither from the heart nor from the mind. Happy now?"

"All your answers are being recorded. So don't try to please me. We have to come to a conclusion. I will analyze in the thesis."

"Yes, I am saying what is coming to my mind at first thought."

"What do you mean by this first thought? Explain in a little more detail."

"The voice of conscience, this is the concept that I believe. I mean from the heart, like the first ray, virgin thinking. Everything changes over time as if there is no conscience, only a manufactured thought according to immediate lust."

"So far, so good, now my next question is, did you feel that way from two or three decades ago, or today?"

"No, it wasn't like that before."

"What was it before?"

"As children, we never felt gender complex. Even our grandparents didn't feel it. So you can't say I was a little kid; that's why I'm probably not a victim of the gender complex."

"What was that time of your age when you start thinking differently?" Laila looked at me with sharp eyes and sipped.

"I was very young in my sixties. As a child, We boys and girls used to play together, till midnight. Only babies. Every girl in the village was considered a sister. Getting married to any girl in the village is like getting married to one's sister. Everyone did the wedding work responsibly. The woman was never seen in any of the girls; only the sister was seen. The enemy also respected the son-in-law of the village."

"It's a little different than us."

"What's the difference?"

"Why the sister understood when she was not your sister at all. It's as if a gender complex was still functioning in your culture at that time. Why don't you consider friends the opposite sex? Does being a friend mean something else?"

"It simply came to our notice then. It was taught from the beginning that the girl from the village is your sister, probably because there was only one whip."

Laila had turned on her laptop and was taking notes at the same time.

"OK, I'll write a note, but the issue is still complicated. It is the easiest way to avoid the appearance of a woman.

Such a relationship is just a shield. It is a matter of informing oneself. It is also easy to guess that the one who is not called a sister is just a woman for you."

"You would have concluded, Laila. I'm saying the same thing, like an open book."

"Let's move on to the second question. My second question is that this phenomenon is no more, I know. Why not now? What are the reasons for this? Have you ever thought about that?"

"Yes, you are right. Not so now. I don't know the reason, but we don't trust each other now. It's not warm relation now."

"Exactly, handsome. There are many reasons for this, some basic and some bare ground, which we will discuss later. The problem is that this complex has made our society sick, and this phenomenon is now becoming global. Only a few villages survive. These villages are inhabited all over the world. The theme of my thesis is how this complex can be diluted."

"Laila, you are asking so much. I will not be able to answer any of your other questions unless you tell me about yourself. I also need to find out what is behind this serious topic? Who are you?"

"It only came to my notice when we met for the first time. It guarantees you to be the right person. I'm glad you asked."

"All you know about me is that I am a rural woman working in a shipping company."

"Before I say anything about myself, let me tell you why this gender complex is born."

"Very interesting!" I said in surprise.

"There is so much happiness in this world. About which we either do not know, or we turn away. You can also see it with sympathy. According to you, when a girl from the village plays with you, she is a child. When she is no longer a child, you start looking for a sister in her, while a person is sitting in her who can give you a lot of happiness.

This emptiness fills you inside and out, and you leave a happy trail.

When there is no play, jumping, having fun, then the happiness buried in the mind, only the lust for a woman goes on the path of digging. It is a sick game.

I am not saying that it is unnecessary, but this need should not be so strong that it swallows the rest of your happiness. Your partner can be anyone.

You can quadruple your happiness by doubling any of its joy, and then gender comes in front of you as a person.

In a nutshell, the warmth of acquaintance turns into the heat of a woman. What you don't want, but you still do. You don't know what you want."

"Laila, I've never heard of such a thing before."

"I lived in Toronto as a child. I was about five years old when my parents were killed in a car accident. I had an uncle, my dad's younger brother. He took me to him, and he admitted me to the school. Uncle was five years younger than my dad and loved his brother very much. Because of this love, he decided that he would only take care of me and never get married. I also forgot my mom and dad because of my uncle's love. Uncle is everything to me.

When I was in grade ten, my uncle had a stroke, and he was permanently confined to a wheelchair. His disability could not support both of us. Uncle never said anything but my age and love for Uncle made me think. It was now my duty to take care of my uncle.

To me, this duty was related to my soul. I also lied to my uncle about what I was thinking about now. The world is not what it should be for me. In any case, I have to take care of Uncle, no matter what I have to do.

At first, I needed money a lot of money. Continually connecting with my surroundings and thinking about what to do. Then one day I saw a job in Chatham. The restaurant owners wanted a female bartender, and it was mentioned that the tip is excellent; I applied, and their reply came. I think it was the right decision for me. Uncle will get a chance to live his life that was not available in my presence. Second, my burden will not be on Uncle, and Third, I will continue my studies with money. Uncle didn't object, and I came to Chatham.

The restaurant was by the lake, facing four streets. There were houses all around and some small lots on which houses were yet to be built, but it seemed that the city was not in a hurry to build more homes. Around the town, various signs signaled the city to be alive. There were plastic gym and outdoor grills outside the houses indicating that people lived inside, training bikes, motorbikes, picnic tables, and motorboats parked somewhere in the yard. Other people could not be called city dwellers. Like the students, the old hippies who used to find drugs around and leave the city whenever they felt like it. Some homes were costly, and some were very cheap."

"Could Uncle have come along or not?" I asked. Now wanting to know the reason behind my question, Laila asked, "Chandan, if you were in my place, would you bring Uncle with you?"

"Yes, this is our tradition. I would keep Uncle with me."

"You would think so, I knew. My thinking is different.

Our Toronto housing townhouses all low class. Most welfare or low income. Our neighbor is a Vietnamese woman who is very friendly with my uncle. Occasionally, she even cooks for my uncle when I'm not home. I wanted to give them some privacy; maybe Uncle would be happy with that.

The second reason for the Chatham move was that I also wanted to study. By the way, I used to come to Toronto every other weekend so that my uncle would not feel lonely and I could even guess about his life. In Chatham, he would have been left alone, he would have been with me, but he would not have been of the same age. The atmosphere in Chatham was different. Later I saw that my decision proved to be right.

"OK, but I think if he were my uncle, he would still be angry with me." It, too, is probably part of the culture. Please tell, what's the story Chatham next."

"Wait, it looks like the recording tape is gone; let's change that."

"Lucy's house is in my heart, where I started coming and going." Laila changed the side of the tape and resumed recording.

The wooden house, which was eight cubits in size, had eight doors. But four of them remained closed forever. Three rooms in the house always closed, I never looked into them, not even dusting, I was not allowed. Two of them always open when a guest comes to the house. The third room belonged to Debbie. Debbie was married and lived in the Kitchener with her fiancée. Still, this room in the house belonged to her and remained hers forever. She stayed in this room whenever she came. Even when she would have come, I would not have made the place clean. I never found out the secret. Only George once said that Debbie had an emotional connection to her room. George didn't even mention why."

"Who was this George?" I asked.

"My first boyfriend."

"Does Michael know?"

"Yes, definably, he is my husband. I told Michael about George before the wedding."

"Mr. and Mrs. Lapre is very old now. They have their daughters and sons. Everybody comes on every Christmas. Michael and I go.

, only at, then"

"Will George come too?"

"What you are thinking is right. Michael and George are good friends."

"This house of the Lapper family is unique, alive ... in my mind. A statue of a civilization. The house is over a hundred years old. It is a joint decision of the family that this house will never be sold.

Even if everyone goes somewhere to live their lives, but everyone comes here at Christmas. This tradition, before my eyes, has been going on for the last thirty years. Now I am a part of it. I am the only one who does not have a blood relationship with the family, yet I have become a part of it. This house seems to me to be my own parent's house. Two old boats, two motorbikes, become a child's play whenever they visit."

"This house is about half a kilometer from Trevor Snack and Bar. It was at this Snack & Bar that I started my job. It is located at Dead End, with a lake behind it. This lake is very bright in summer. People come to celebrate the holidays. The bar at this picnic spot, though moderate, is full of bright weather. I would come back from school at three o'clock, put on my uniform here, and start work at four o'clock. My shift was until eleven o'clock at night. I was housed in a small room in the basement."

"Before going to school in the morning, I used to jog by the lake for half an hour; sometimes, I enjoyed jogging barefoot in the sand. It was during this jog that I first met George. Hi Casual. Later, George and his family came to our restaurant, and I served them. They also gave me a ten-dollar tip. At that time, an end of ten dollars seemed like a considerable amount. I said no, but when Lucy told me to keep it, I couldn't say no. George started coming and going, and I could see the attraction in his eyes, and it was fine.

He took Lucy's name and invited me to come home, which I accepted."

George took Lucy's name and invited me to come home, which I accepted."

"Did you have that kind of attraction in your heart?" When I asked, Laila said, "Yes, I used to get ecstatic too." On the appointed day, I went to their house. What I liked most was that I was honored as a guest. I had a special dinner. I left work at seven o'clock that day. There was no problem with the hours off on weekdays, but I had to get back to my room by eleven o'clock. Night cleaning was also my responsibility.

As a guest, this was the first experience of my life, which was very pleasant.

as I was leaving, Lucy said, "You are only a guest today; you have to come as a member of the house for the future." He also gave the phone number so that whenever there is any problem, you can call home, whoever is in the house will come to your aid and don't feel alone. Only a mother can give so much love to her daughter, and my mother died, which makes me very emotional. My eyes filled with tears. I didn't sleep well that night, and I missed my uncle a lot."

"It simply came to our notice then. Many moments of life are forever in our mind." I said.

"Do you remember anything, such a moment spent?" Laila asked.

"Yes, there are many, but now I don't know what to say to match your moment."

"No matter what you say, the effect is the same for everyone. Any moment that makes my eyes water."

"Yes, at the moment, I only remember Sunil's words."

"Who is Sunil?"

"My wife, we were newly married, and I was a refugee. No one knew. What to do, but after marriage, there was hope. Sunil had deposited her money in the joint account. Twenty thousand dollars was not a small amount. Because of the arranged marriage, we have not yet formed a cordial relationship. Even though Sunil's money belonged to the family, it made my eyes water."

"She must be great. These are the moments I am looking for, for my thesis project. It is also important for you to know what you think about the need for marriage. Did you know Sunil before?"

"No, this relationship was arranged by my uncle; the only purpose was to settle in Canada."

"Come on, it makes sense to you, but why did Sunil marry you?" Did she mean anything?"

"No, that doesn't make sense. After all, girls are married off by our parents. Now kids want to do whatever they want."

"I understand, but I have seen in other cases that such marriages later reunite the souls, and sometimes even the proposed marriages fail."

"Let's go ahead and listen," I said.

"I was in a dilemma for a while after meeting George.

My curiosity was now focused on what happened next instead of understanding the point. That's when I thought of my daughter Bunty once or twice, but soon after Laila's words, I would come back to the motel room again.

"George's sister Debbie built a custom home in Kitchener, and everyone was going, and I was invited. I was thinking, can't make a decision. After all, it was their family event when George called the restaurant owner and took leave for me. I worked for two years and was eighteen now, but I was very serious, much more than my age. I would weigh everything. I only had a friendship with George; he had not yet become my boyfriend. I was waiting for him to say something one day.

When he came home, he would drop me off at eleven o'clock at night, waiting for me to say something. We drank coffee in one place, parked the car in a dark corner, but what I was waiting for was not said, nor did he say anything else. At that age, sitting with George, my limbs would stiffen, and waves would rise. I wish George would hug me. I later learned that this was the tradition of the family. That was the level of my friendship with Lucy and George.

I was sitting in a parked car, sipping coffee, thinking of getting fit. George talks about ice hockey. I was asking questions about my studies. Asking which subject to go to next, but what I was thinking would not happen. Sometimes I would get upset, my limbs would get irritated, but George never reached them. George was scheduled to go to Windsor to study architecture, and he was scheduled to leave in September, the year Debbie built the house."

"Lucy built this house for Debbie with money from the estate. The money belonged to the family, but no one interfered with Debbie and her hubby."

On his way back from Kitchener, George parked his car at a truck stop on the highway and expressed his love for me for the first time. I want you to take the key to that new house from my mom, as Debbie took it Today."

"I didn't tell George, but in my heart, I thought I was a poor girl with an uncle. Will George allow Uncle to stay in our house? Will the uncles agree to stay in George's house? These questions were very true and bitter, but those were my questions, the solution to which was as important as loving George, and then what would be the choice? I didn't say anything to George at the time, but I decided not to accept the proposal until I had decided. George just proposed, leaving the decision to me."

"It would have been nice for Uncle, too, a clean environment," I said.

"No, Chandan, maybe you still can't figure out how much and where is the sensitivity in my words?" Uncle was full of self-respect, who also took the divine decision as a challenge. I couldn't ask him anything. If Uncle knows even a crack of it, he will do everything in his control for my happiness. Even he has to leave me for a long time. I have to think about everything myself.

"You have a perfect family; these emotions are family," I said.

"Yes, you are right. We are from Newfoundland. I don't know anything about my family; one of my aunts lives in New York. Sometimes she comes to see me once or twice a year, but her mind doesn't get wet with me. She thinks that the uncle doesn't think of anything because of me. She has a brother, I understand her way of thinking, but she couldn't connect with me. Uncle's thoughts tell me how much my family will be honored."

"I'm obsessed with your story, I don't want to jump in, but I'm still desperate to know the truth; what happened next?"

"I took time off from George. He explained his plans. With the subject of architecture, he aspired to be a great realtor but stayed around Chatham. He would be confused by my Toronto move, and I didn't want to create this confusion for him. When my brain stops working, and you know who helped me?"

"No, when you are telling me everything strange, every character is ideal, how can I guess, you tell me."

"Lucy. When my brain stopped working, I talked to Mom Lucy. In front of everyone, I called Lucy Mom, and Mr. Lapre called his wife Mom, too, in front of everyone. She was the mother of all; now, she is very old. Uncle Lapper passed away two years ago."

"What did you say to Lucy?" I asked curiously.

"I took Mom Lucy to the lake for talk. After hearing all this, Mom Lucy said, "I have many losses, but I will not talk about myself." I can't find a daughter-in-law like you, but I would think of Uncle too if I were in your place. These are our traditions. Don't even talk to your uncle about it; decide for yourself. If your decision is different from mine, I will be personally happy, but it will hurt the traditions. My mind was fixed. I thanked Mom Lucy and said that I should not be late and move to Toronto soon. Otherwise, it would be too late. If my heart is lost, so will George's, but the sooner he finds out the truth, the better."

"Then quit your job?"

"Yes, I had to leave. After all, I had to leave Chatham for higher studies in September, and George wanted me to move to Windsor, but I came to Toronto and took care of my room."

"Indeed, this was your ideal decision, Laila."

"Yes, Chandan, you talked about ideal character. Let me tell you, If you are positive, everybody around you must be ideal. God does it purposely."

The uncle was also pleased to see me back. Michael used to come to Uncle's friend Tia for tutoring, which I got to know Michael. Shortly after the date, Michael proposed to me.

I told Michael all about my problem, Uncle George and Lucy, and I accepted his proposal and saw his smile. During this time, George's phone calls kept coming. Gradually, George's phone stopped ringing. Mom Lucy explained to him my compulsion step by step. George was my 'best man' at our wedding."

"George also got married. For the past couple of months, Debbie and George have asked me to come to Chatham for a while. Mom Lucy is ancient, it's time to leave, and her leave should be good. They want to build a memorial for her in Chatham. Lucy has shares in a shipping company, so my job was arranged

The whole family, including me, has decided to build a library in the name of Mom Lucy and to keep all of Lucy's books in it. The project is due to be completed on September 19, which is Mommy Lucy's birthday. It will be a gift for Mom Lucy. I have also come to Chatham to take part in it. Michael is with me.

Michael says, let's settle here, but our decision is not yet as long as the uncles live. See what happens in the future. Today, George and Michael are working together on this project. There is also a room for Michael, who will provide free tutoring to the children around the neighborhood."

"Great Laila, this is just great; I wish I could think the same way." Our traditions are also vibrant."

"But now they are thin," Laila said.

"Yes, but how do you know?"

"In my project, I have studied the traditions of the nations. Your nation's traditions are very similar to those of Mom Lucy's nation; they are Polish. Mom Lucy came to Canada with her dad and was a farmer in Poland. I don't know about the previous dynasty, but now their dynasty has started in the name of Lucy Mom. All the waxes consider Lucy their ancestor, and follow in her footsteps. Their fourth generation was born in Canada."

"We don't know much about Punjabi about the history of nations. Yes, only a few scholars know. Of course, they should come forward, but it is not visible yet. Many, like me, are still searching for the cause of domestic violence. It is a short cut to curbing domestic violence. Recognize your heritage, know your traditions, work on real causes. This domestic violence will end automatically. Laila, can you help me?"

"Yes, why not?" Even though we are divided into nations, we are one. Sensors, claimants of traditions, builders of rules, I will help you if you help yourself."

"Yes, of course, today you have opened my eyes."

"I know Chandan, but you tell me yourself," Laila said with a smile, and I understood that now it is my turn. Laila will fry my thinking in her pan."

"What?"

"What did you think when you came here to me in the motel?"

"What do you think?"

"No, you tell me. I know."

"Meet you, gossip," Laila screamed and laughed at me.

"I tell you, you came to sleep with me. You may also think that my hubby also knows my immorality, and we are very wild in this matter. You come, we'll drink whiskey, and then ..."

"Yes, Laila, I will not lie; that's what I thought."

"Now, tell me about Sunil; what would she think when you are not home at night?" Only that you must be involved in some critical work. And she will not have any superstition about that vital work either."

"Laila, it's too much. Do you think we're all cheap?"

"No, not everyone, not even you, not even Sunil." Your behavior has given me this idea."

"How is that?"

"Look, when we met, you never mentioned your wife's name. You could also say that we went home when I talked about staying in a motel. Not even mentioning your house's name, it was told what kind of atmosphere there is in your house. If it were Michael or me, we would never do that;

yes, if you still asked me to stay in the motel, I could easily understand that it is your choice. I had no interest in spending dollars on motels."

"It simply came to me about your privacy. Don't you believe it?"

"No," Let's face it, Chandan, what about the third eye of a woman?" No matter what the nation is, a woman is subconsciously aware of what the person in front thinks."

"Let's just say this. But why does this aspect of a man's thinking arise? Can't an ordinary person guess what happened to me as I did?"

"That's the gender complex; anyone can guess the action of a male friend on their own?

"Not possible, right?" Laila said

"Today is your day Laila, whatever you said, is right."

"Then what is the need to guess about the woman?" Don't answer, I tell you. This phenomenon starts with the unconscious and develops. There are thousands of interests in the world. A balance has to be struck.

Tremendous confidence is self-confidence. When you talk about your inner woman, you understand why the interests are churning in the woman only. There is no way out of life. Life has to be lived. When we don't even live life, then most things in our minds dictate to us. It is where the gender complex starts.

We should get involved in sports, books, literature, or any social activity and get some peace from it. Your vacation is communicated to Sunil; your complexes will be affected.

; in this case, women's thinking is more grey than men's. I am not talking about you, but I am talking about totality."

"Laila, tell me what it means to be together in a motel at night, isn't it an invitation?" Both accept such invitations. Did you believe me that I think the way you think?

"No, I didn't trust you. There are many other times when I don't trust my male friends. But it doesn't matter to me. I believe in myself, and that is enough. I need to talk to someone and change their thinking; I am not usually the one who handles that. I say what I believe. My project, as well as being academic, is my own. I undertake any project only when I believe in it. What effect does this meeting have on you? Whether it happens or not, I have nothing to do with it. When you said that you too are working on domestic violence in Punjabi culture, I was eager to know your culture in detail."

"I understand your viewpoint."

"Doesn't it feel like a waste of time?"

"No, Laila, you have taught me to think differently. My life revolves around a few points. Nothing is being achieved, but the complications are increasing day by day."

"OK. Chandan, it is morning now. It's three o'clock. I have to go to bed now. Hit the last two pegs. If you want to sleep here too, you can."

"No, Laila, I have to go home now. I will sleep for four hours, then again routine life, but I promised to think of something new now. I'm having problems at home too."

"OK, good night or good morning, whatever." Whenever I wake up, I will leave for Chatham. I will call and hope that next time I come to Toronto; I will come to your house and meet Sunil. I don't know why she seems to be my friend."

I picked up the car keys, waved my hand, and walked out. It was four o'clock when I got home. I drank coffee on the way. When I got home, I slept on the mats in the living room without knocking. I wake up with the noise coming from the kitchen,

Hearing my voice, Sunil said, "Wait a minute. I bring tea for you." Do you have to drink lemonade too?" She knew that whenever I spent the night outside, I had a headache in the morning.

"No, I will drink only tea."

Taking a cup of tea, Sunil played the DVD of the serial. I jokingly asked, "Did your Bhabi in the serial get the necklace?"

"Yes, the necklace has been found. In fact, the necklace was not lost. It was very protective. There was a lot of noise, and the whole episode was spent trying to find the necklace."

"You look thrilled, Sunil. Did you find any of your lost necklaces?"

"Yes, I am thrilled. Today. It's like finding a necklace."

"Don't you want to tell me?"

"I am very excited to tell you. That is why I make noises in the kitchen to wake you up. I talked to Bunty last night."

"What time did Bunty come home?"

"She came before twelve. Dominic gave her ride home."

"And what's so happy about that?"

"Yes, I do. When I saw Dominic, I became very hyper, and I decided to deal with Bunty Today. I sat next to her on the couch. Perhaps she, too, understood the mother's pain. I cried while talking. Seeing me crying, Bunty got up, gave me some water, hugged me, and said, Don't know what you keep thinking? Look, even though I'm a girl, I still have friends. How can I let go of my friends?"

"You don't know what's going on these days? There are rapes every day."

"Mom, I am not alone on the streets. Dominic is with me, and he is also a boxer. Does anyone want to force me?"

"But that's what I'm afraid. Dominic will hurt you sexually one day, then leave you alone, or one day you will say I want to marry him; what will we show people?"

"Mom, there is no such thing. I love you; I understand your traditions. I will never do anything that will hurt you. You have a great place in my life. I think our rituals bound marriage. And this Dominic is not my boyfriend; he is just a friend. We have been studying together since childhood. Why don't you understand? He also has a girlfriend.

She is also my friend. She is also Italian. I go to their houses but do not call them home.

You just hang everything on the same nail."

"It means your necklace was found too."

"Yes, you have become a philosopher."

"Yes, sometimes."